# Svevi Avatar Glimpses

## THE PANDEMIC BEGINS

### A NOVELLA

# Svevi Avatar Glimpses

## THE PANDEMIC BEGINS

A NOVELLA

Maya Svevak

IGUANA

Copyright @ 2020 Maya Svevak
Published by Iguana Books
720 Bathurst Street, Suite 303
Toronto, ON  M5S 2R4

Publisher: Meghan Behse
Editor: Lee Parpart
Proofreader: Amanda Feeney
Cover design: Palash Das

ISBN 978-1-77180-459-2 (paperback)
ISBN 978-1-77180-460-8 (epub)
ISBN 978-1-77180-461-5 (Kindle)

This is an original print edition of *Svevi Avatar Glimpses: The Pandemic Begins,* the novella.

## Dedication

Dedicated to the millions of human beings
whose lives were devastated by the Coronavirus pandemic,

simply for

trying to feed their families,
walking home to their towns and villages,
having dark skin,
seeking refuge from poverty and violence,
being jailed while innocent,
falling into the manipulative trap of an abusive lover,
exercising their civil rights, and
trying to stop the escalating rape of our earth.

# EVOLUTION

# GLIMPSES OF THE BEGINNING

*Time.*

*How you torture me in your countless manifestations. You are the past, the future, and also the present. On occasion, you barely crawl, then suddenly you begin sprinting. I am a leaf caught in the gales of your willfulness. You have imprisoned me here in this moment of grave consequence for all of humanity. If only you would let me remain here. Instead, I feel channels into the past tugging at me, entreating me to leave the present. You may be teeming with more power than even space. But I shall not allow you to toy with me.*

*I must resist. I must not leave.*

*Why do you burden me with experiences from another chain of time? Men annihilating the innocent with their weapons. Nuclear detonations in mushroom clouds. Spanish conquistadors on horseback. Forces of destruction drawn by chariots and elephants. How relieved I am that that chain of time perished! The imperialists never gained power. Humanity was not made to suffer those atrocities. So why, time, must you continually remind me of the horrors that occurred elsewhen, even though I am no longer gripped by this other chain of Cause and Effect that diverged long ago?*

*Now here I sit at this long, forbidding table, among these leaders, in the capital of a land vastly different from what I know it could have been. What shall be their choice? Never before, within the bounds of their awareness, have they stood at such a precipice. Shall they choose* destruction or peace? Five years ago, they destroyed almost all of their people — a fact that is finally resurfacing.

Qingshan.

Fear grips her tightly. Suddenly I sense her memories. They draw me in. I try to resist invading her mind with mine. But despite the extent of my powers, there are occasions when I cannot control them. My mind intrudes upon her thoughts. They dwell on those crucial moments from five years ago. How lucky she is that her past is firmly behind her, not to be relived. That her memories are merely thoughts that can be retrieved when she desires to do so. I am not so fortunate. Time, why do you single me out with your unkindness, while you treat others with compassion?

With great difficulty, I sever my mind from hers. I look around this circular room, a room that endows its elected occupant with so much power. Across from and beside me are twelve men and women, most of their faces in the shadows. As though light itself were ashamed to illuminate them. They are arguing, wrestling over falsehoods and insecurities. In this moment, Qingshan appears to be more severely affected by their bickering than any other at this table. Her remembered anxiety beckons me again. I try to resist, but my attempts are futile. The harrowing agitation consuming her face pulls me away from this Meeting of Conclusions. My mind is ensnared by hers. You mock me, time, in my moment of weakness. You collude with her agonized recollections to create a channel within you into the past. You reel me in through her memories. I must not allow my mind to journey back. Yet, against my will, you draw me into her past.

Your flow is fragmenting, time.

I am being pulled into your shards.

Past and present are merging.

An insurmountable heaviness. I am incapacitated, unable to fight you, for as a body and mind defined by time and space, I am helplessly bound within you. I am at your mercy, time, even though you have none. My body remains at this table. Yet my thoughts, my identity have been immersed in Qingshan of five years and one day ago. The day after *the autumnal equinox. Qingshan, I apologize for my essence merging into yours. I am unable to restrain myself.*

*My identity as Maya slips away as it takes on Qingshan's of the past. Yet my metamorphosis does not stop there. Despite my efforts to hold onto my own essence, it transforms into that of another being.*

*I am no longer Maya of the present. I am an alien being within Qingshan of the past.*

What are these strange new surroundings? Will I survive here? Alone in this foreign place with no one to guide me? Moments ago I was nestled comfortably in my host of thousands of years, secure in the knowledge that I would thrive. I know that they do not consider me to be animate. Yet I live. I assemble my mind and body from the building blocks of life. I multiply and I propagate. If that is not being alive, then what is? I am smaller than any living being, yet so much more powerful.

*My essence has not been lost entirely. I am still aware of being Maya. Yet I am also a mighty virus. My metamorphosis is unstable; I am swayed by the pained longings of the virus for its past. For the surroundings that comforted it for countless generations. My identity transforms once more.*

*Now I am the previous host of the virus, a nectar bat flying high above the earth, carrying the virus within.*

How wonderful, this feeling of lightness. I am as unburdened as the clouds, as agile as the winds. How I love soaring on the breeze with the sun warming my wings. How I revel in gliding over the mountains that have been my solace since childhood. How I adore the ancient river watering the fields that have fed us since time immemorial. My wife warned me not to venture out in daylight. But what choice did I have? Our traditional sources of food have dwindled.

I am hungry. It has been so long since I have had a sweet drink of nectar from my favorite field of flowers. With sadness I approach the winding river and the banks that rely on her kindness, for I know what sight awaits me. The vibrant petals of yellow and red and blue have abandoned us. I help to pollinate the plants and spread their seeds. So why are they dying? Their leaves and stems are brown and wilted. And why does the river look so dull? I have wondered for some time now why it no longer looks as blue as it once did, why it no longer glistens. How gruesome, those floating, bloated dead bodies of fish that frolicked so joyfully before. Smoky streams of disease are burdening the winding river from the north.

Even though I am weak from hunger, I must follow the river upstream. Today I must know from where this sickness comes. So many nights and days have passed as I have searched for food in vain. The forests and fields that have kept my family alive for thousands of years no longer give us what we need. I dread what awaits me up north, for the winding river below me becomes ever darker and more dismal.

Never before have I been here. The river of my youth joins with another, larger river that bends toward the east. What is that smoking patch of hemorrhaged earth where the two rivers meet? What a terrible sight. What an intolerable stench. I see and smell a gargantuan beast. Its thousand mouths belching out thick black smoke. Its rotting bowels spewing noxious excrement into the rivers. Those humans must have built this lifeless monstrosity. This plague they call a city. They pour death into the waters and the lands. I am suffocating here. I must turn back.

As I fly southward, back toward my home, my thoughts dwell on my family. Yesterday I watched as my mother died of starvation. I had nothing to give her, not even a morsel of hope. Helplessly I wrapped my wings around her quivering body and felt the trembling subside as she slipped into lifelessness.

How can any living being generate so much waste that it kills everything around it? Do the humans have no understanding of the symbiosis between water and food? Between soil and plants? Between plants and animals? Do they not understand that to ensure life for one's children, one must take only what one needs and give as much in return?

Today I must find food to feed my family, for my heart is already weak from hunger and grief. I will not survive the agony of watching another one of my blood dwindling into death. Will I need to venture farther south beyond the river and fields that have always sustained us?

As I fly beyond the sleeping caverns that are my home, I suddenly see dwellings along the eastern bank of the river. Perhaps those humans who settled near the mountains have food? Not so long ago, there were no humans. And then the pale men made their nest here. As I approach their settlement, I wonder at the curious shapes of their dwellings. They are made of earth and wood and molded into cubes and cuboids with sharp corners. How strange that they have cut down all of the trees inside their nest. There is barely a patch of green anywhere. Wait, as I fly further south, where the dwellings are farther apart, I see a garden.

At long last! Flowers that are not dead or dying like in the fields.

Yet those flowers, they look familiar. Indeed, they are the same as the flowers that grow deep in the mountain forests. But how did these wild plants get here? They do not belong here, exposed to the winds of the plains. Something is wrong. There is danger here. I sense it. I should leave. Yet my family is starving. I must imbibe so that I can feed my children this nectar. I must drink to strengthen myself, for I have grown almost too weak to fly.

I alight on the delicate petals of a particularly bright yellow flower and drink deeply from its womb. Such delightful sweetness this blossom harbors in its depths. I taste such joy.

Why is that human woman suddenly rushing toward me in such anger? Have I offended her in some way? Does she not know that I will serve this plant in return for taking its nectar? She is shouting at me, her arm raised to strike me. I will stay just a bit longer to gather more nectar for my children before I leave. Just a moment more.

*As Qingshan's hand strikes down my weary bat body, emaciated from hunger, I once more sense my identity as Maya for a split second, mingled with that of the bat. What excruciating pain! How can she be so cruel? Why would she punish my bat self for trying to fend off my family's starvation? Life ebbs from my bat body. But as Maya I am not to find peace in the lap of death. I cannot escape as the heaviness paralyzes me yet again. I am Maya for only the briefest of moments before my essence transforms once more.*

*I have again become that same virus within Qingshan.*

My poor bat host. He has been injured and killed by this human woman merely for feeding his hunger. Had she not bled while striking him, I would not have been able to flow from him to her. Never before have I left the warmth of the bat, my home for thousands of years. What a strangely unfamiliar host this human is. What a peculiar smell arises from her blood. I will have to learn anew how to multiply and prosper — for the first time, within a human.

*Suddenly, without warning, you catapult me from the past back into the dark room in the capital. How inconsiderate you are, time. For I know that the present affords me a safe harbor for only a moment. I have reclaimed my essence as Maya from the virus and find myself sitting in the Governor's Mansion once more, among these leaders who hold the fate of humanity in their hands.*

*And so, the pandemic began five years ago. With Qingshan, who did not even know what had found a new home within her. She sits quietly at one end of the long table, the only Chin person in this ominous room. It would be better if she were not present here at this Meeting of Conclusions. Bitter words of the recent pandemic agitate her most vehemently. So much so that her anxiety resonates with my own emotions and thoughts. I try to resist being drawn into her mind, into the whirlwind of disquiet that makes it impossible for her thoughts to remain in the present.*

*The virus within Qingshan of five years ago beckons me most fervently. And so I find my essence transforming itself once more. I begin losing my grasp over my identity as Maya. Even within this being that exists at the edge of life and non-life, I am helplessly trapped in its perception of time. One month from when the bat perished passes by in less than a blink. My identity becomes that of the virus on the Day of Bereavement, five years ago.*

## CHAPTER ONE

# THE PORTAL'S REVELATION

*I am the virus within the body of Qingshan of almost five years ago.*

Where is my new host going today? She is stepping off of a boat onto the western bank of the winding river. She walks along a steep cliff protruding out from the side of the old mountains. A crowd is gathered in the distance. Why are all these humans congregating here? This place, it smells familiar. I recognize it. It is the entrance to the sleeping caverns of my previous bat host.

I remember well the journey into and out of the cave when I was still within the nectar bat. A long and rocky tunnel leads into the bowels of the mountain, opening onto a spectacular grotto. The large, musky hollow is adorned with imposing stalactites dripping mysteriously from the ceiling and striated stalagmites rising majestically from the ground. This hallowed place is where the ancestors of my previous bat host built their refuge so long ago.

I can sense them sleeping in the caverns that have kept them safe for centuries.

How I yearn for their moist familiarity. How I miss my bat host gliding joyously into the winds upon rushing out of the tunnel. I can still sense his rapture at smelling the crisp air and the wispy clouds each evening. These humans, they say that this is a groundbreaking ceremony for a new coal mine. But what will happen to the bats if the humans invade their home and begin to destroy it? What will happen to their ancient and harmonious way of life?

This new host is so foreign to me. The journey from one end of her to the other is long. Even though she is taller and bigger than my previous bat host, in many ways she is less capable. Her ears do not enable her to navigate her surroundings using sound. And her hands are merely hands. They are not wings that allow her to glide on the clouds far above the earth to revel in the glory of solitude.

But nostalgia serves no purpose. I must focus on my survival in this new host. In these past few days, I have adapted and multiplied sufficiently to fill her lungs. Each time she exhales, each time she coughs, my progeny leave her body through tiny droplets of water. Another human woman is walking toward my host, just as my host begins coughing. She is tall and pale, with wavy brown tresses and piercing green eyes.

"You have no business here, Chin!" the other human shouts. She steps close to my host, threatening, aggressive, practically towering over her.

My host coughs once more, sending thousands of aqueous particles into the air. Each one inhabited by countless numbers of my progeny. Here is my opportunity to spread myself to another. For a brief moment I hover in a water droplet suspended between the two humans. And then I dissolve into the tongue of the other woman.

I have paved the path for my progeny to thrive inside other humans.

The blood of my new host tastes different than that of my host with the straight black hair. How strange, the appearance of these humans. Even though they are almost identical inside, their shells are shaped and colored in myriad forms and hues.

My new host is oblivious to my presence.

She continues to yell at the black-haired human. "What are you doing on this side of Constantina? This is not where your kind should be."

"What are you talking about?" the smaller one says, annoyed.

"You know exactly what I'm talking about, Chin."

This word seems to anger the one with the long black hair. "I have a name, Europan," she bristles. "And that name is Doctor Qingshan Han."

"I don't care what the demon your name is. You have no right to be here. This mine belongs to Cardiff."

"No right to be here? What are you talking about? I'm conducting research at the Cardiff Institute of Horticulture."

My new host laughs, a cruel sound, devoid of humor. "You expect me to believe that a Chin can conduct research?"

"The ignorance of your kind never ceases to amaze me, Europan."

"Show me your papers."

"I am a Constantinan citizen. I'm under no obligation to show you anything at all."

"The demon you're not!" my new host hisses, taking another step closer to my previous host.

My progeny swirl in the air between them, as if playing a game of hide and seek between the two humans, entering one and then jumping back to the other.

"What's your problem?" my previous host demands to know.

"My problem is you people. You think you can just go wherever you like and do whatever you want in this country that my people built with their own sweat and labor."

"My people saved you when you were on the brink of annihilating yourselves."

"Utter nonsense. That's what you tell yourselves to feel like you matter."

"Is that so? And how do you matter?"

My new host — the one the dark-haired woman calls Europan — is taken aback. I can feel the blood pumping more rapidly through her veins.

"Beatrice matters," she says through gritted teeth. "I matter. Don't you ever dare question that!"

Their argument catches the ears of some other humans who are congregating nearby, in front of the square entrance to the cave. All of those humans are pale, like my new host. They begin advancing threateningly toward the black-haired human.

*Suddenly, the past releases me from its beguiling hold. Time, how you disorient me. Again, I become aware of being in the present. I am no longer the virus; I am Maya once more. But my body is still reacting to the panic that had begun to suffuse poor Qingshan when the virus left her. My mind is still linked to hers. How frightened she was when Beatrice and those people surrounded her menacingly. Her remembered anguish echoes deafeningly within me. As those pale men and women closed in on her, Qingshan's characteristic confidence gave way to insecurities about her identity. In those moments, she felt shame for being Chin. In those moments, all of her accomplishments and abilities seemed to fade into futility.*

*Shall these people ever stop shunning those who are different from them? Shall they ever stop destroying what they fear?*

*I manage to tear my thoughts away from Qingshan's and focus once more on the table and the people sitting around it. The men across from me avoid my gaze. The older ones because they believe that I am insignificant and therefore not worth acknowledging. The younger ones because they are too busy attempting to hide that they are fidgeting. Except for four of us, none of the men and women seated at this table had anticipated being called upon to decide the fate of humanity. And so they breathe nervous uncertainty into the stale air between us.*

*My eyes wander to the far end of the table and immediately freeze on Qingshan's face. Fear emanates from her, ensnaring me once more. I close my eyes in an attempt to break the connection I do not want. It is to no avail. Her mind molds mine as it continues to dwell on her feelings of alienation from that day when she first met Beatrice. That day when she, unbeknownst to her, initiated the first human-to-human spread of the virus that nearly wiped out the people of Constantina. When Beatrice questioned her right to be at the mine that is attributed to Cardiff, one of the oldest settlements of the Europans and the only one on the banks of the Shenandoa River, Qingshan felt unseen. She was overcome by alternating waves of indignation and self-doubt, succeeded by tides of terror as a crowd of Europan descendants closed in on her.*

*I apologize once more, Qingshan, for resonating with your mind without your permission. But your remembered despair begs me not to forsake it. I cannot ignore such a call. For I, too, have known the angry helplessness you recall so vividly.*

# CHAPTER TWO

# DECEPTION THROUGH CONTROL

## FAVORITISM

*Bunim sits on the other side of the table, his left palm cradling his limp right hand. The head of his wooden walking stick is visible next to his left elbow, just above the surface of the sterile plastic table. Am I, Maya, projecting my own sense of foreboding onto him? Or am I truly observing despair in the way his ample mustache is drooping? My eyes fixate on his. I have more than an inkling of why the despair of others, whether imagined or not, compels me with such fervor. But now is not the time for my flaws to assert themselves. Time. You suspend yourself during my forays into the minds and bodies of others. Whether it is a moment or an entire year that has passed while I am experiencing the reality of the past from within another, not even a new breath has been taken in the present my body inhabits.*

*You can be so vexing! I feel your attempts to amuse yourself at my expense. All the little games you play — the sense impressions that turn out to be illusions, the compressions and expansions. If not for these manipulations, I should like to explore your marvels and capabilities. Instead, I am consumed by my failure to fathom your true nature. My body molds itself to the boundaries you create for it, yet I do not understand you.*

*My gaze is drawn to Bunim's face again. His amber eyes shimmer in torment. In this moment, the conflict within him surpasses that of anyone else, and so I find my mind moving quickly to embrace his. My teacher taught me that with great power comes an even greater responsibility of restraint. She taught me never to exercise my ability to merge with others without their express permission. If only this potent ability were fully under my control! My ineptitude at restraining myself is shameful. Bunim dwells on the summer solstice of four years ago, eight months after the groundbreaking at the sleeping caverns of the bats. The sun had barely risen in the most affluent quarter of Cardiff. Bunim, I apologize for invading your mind and your body. I cannot control myself. My essence is transforming.*

*I am Bunim of four years ago, standing in the shadows.*

I grip my walking stick more tightly with my left hand to relieve some of the pain in my left thigh. From a nearby balcony, a male voice cuts through the air. Paul Duval, a short, pale-skinned man wearing a translucent head mask with a filter and gloves, just like mine, shouts enthusiastically to a sizeable crowd below.

"It's great to be here in this old town, where Europan values are still cherished," he bellows. "The Governor couldn't be here, but I'm his most trusted man, so you're in the best hands! I'm here to give you what you need."

He has no understanding of what Constantinans need. He has no grasp of the history of our people. He knows nothing about this frontier town. He's young and arrogant, having experienced only wealth and privilege. And yet, the Governor has appointed him his representative during this crisis. The unmasked, ungloved men and women assembled below him in this cul-de-sac hang on his every word. Even though almost a year has passed since the virus outbreak, the government has failed to provide any protection to its citizens. All protective equipment has been reserved for government officials, like me.

"See what's in these hands?" Paul asks smugly, reaching into a tall plastic drum sitting next to him on the balcony. "You guessed right! Masks and gloves to keep the Chin virus away. Here. Catch. There's enough for everyone. You can thank me later."

I lift my right forearm to my face to smooth my mustache through my sturdy syntho mask, avoiding the filter and ignoring my sagging right wrist. Something about that young fool deeply irritates me. When did we begin calling this the Chin virus? It must be an invention of the Governor because I haven't heard the President use this term. I'm certain that those syntho gloves and masks spilling over the rim of that giant plastic drum on the balcony are not of sufficient quality to prevent the virus from spreading among the people. I happen to know that there is a major shortage of protective equipment that's actually effective. Is this simply a publicity stunt on election day? One last attempt to get people to vote for his boss?

The crowd doesn't seem to notice. They are obviously enthralled by the prospect of having any protective equipment at all, no matter how effective it is. Hands reach up eagerly, hoping to be the first to catch any thin gloves and filter-less masks that begin to rain down.

So many faces in this crowd are unfamiliar to me these days. My beloved Cardiff, the town of my birth, has begun to feel foreign. I was born in the same house where my father was born and his father before him. These newcomers from the big cities have little appreciation for our history. Just a few years ago, they burst into our town with their plastic money and bought out the old families who used to inhabit this quarter. They tore down the sturdy buildings that housed many generations of grandmothers and mothers, brothers and sisters. Nothing remains of them now. In their place stand houses bursting with ostentatiousness and opulence, not humility.

This was not the vision of my ancestors. Cardiff was never meant to be a weekend getaway for the rich. It was not built to be a mountainside oasis for the spoiled. These people don't care about my town. They don't care about its founders or their descendants. We take pride in keeping our culture intact here. Our culture of hard work, caring, and collaboration. We take only what we need, something we learned from our allies, without whom we would have perished a long time ago.

What's that boy up to now? He's grabbing handfuls of syntho masks and gloves and throwing them down onto the people, as though they were caged animals in a zoo. He's laughing as though this were all some humorous game. And those silly men and women are obliging him by cheering and catching. Why can't they show more pride? Why are they so dazzled by his hollow gestures?

What's that movement in the back of the crowd? A thin, middle-aged man is trying to get Paul's attention. A Chin man, here in Cardiff, so far down in the southwest? Most of their towns are located in the outskirts of Oniosa, the old industrial city built by the settlers where the Shenandoa River flows out of the Potomac River in the north. We don't usually see Chin in this part of Constantina. I wonder what he's doing here.

"Please, Sir, I take care of my frail, old father," he implores. "He is my only family."

Poor man. He looks so forlorn. What does he want? I see the crowd moving away from him, as though he were a leper. How much longer will we continue to have these types of reactions to people who aren't the same as we are?

"If I become infected, who will take care of him? Please, can I have a mask?"

A young, blond woman pushes herself to the back of the crowd. "Those masks and gloves are for us Constantinans, not for aliens like you!" she declares.

The bigotry of my own people never ceases to amaze me. The pandemic has only aggravated tensions. Two of my men from Security Assuredness and Freedom Enforcement are marching up to the Chin man, hardy syntho masks with protruding filters under their bullet-proof helmets. As one of the men grabs the Chin man's upper arm with his syntho-gloved hand, a stabbing pain jolts my left knee. Clenching my jaw, I grasp my walking stick more firmly and try to move as quickly as I can toward the men. The pain worsens as I pick up speed, but I manage to reach them.

"What has he done that you're hauling him away like this?" I demand with authority.

The SAFE agent temporarily relaxes his grip on the Chin man and faces me. "Sir, this man isn't supposed to be here on election day. All citizens are to be in the towns where they are registered to vote."

"That's *if* they plan to vote, agent," I persist. "As far as I know, the law still regards voting as a discretionary right of citizens, not an obligatory act. If this man wants to be here, he has the right to be here."

"Unless I say otherwise," Paul says, his voice cutting through the sudden silence in the street.

I stop and stare at him. "I beg your pardon?"

"You heard me, Buni."

His insolence triggers another round of nerve pain in my knee.

"My name is Bunim Cardozo, Paul. You may call me Mister Cardozo or Bunim."

"Look, man," Paul shouts from the balcony, ignoring my insistence on being addressed properly, "I'm the Governor's representative. I can order those men to do whatever I want."

"Actually, SAFE is under the jurisdiction of the President, not the Governor," I reply curtly.

Paul sniggers, "Yeah, but not on election day. Tough luck, Buni."

The SAFE agent holding the Chin man looks at me with hesitant confusion.

"Take the Chin away!" Paul orders imperiously. "By authority of the Governor of Constantina."

Several men and women in the crowd begin cheering, and others join them. I glare at them, shocked by their behavior. Why are they so invested in whether this poor Chin man stays or goes? It is beyond my comprehension. I stare impotently at one of the SAFE agents, my eyes drawn to the white panchika imprinted onto a black circular patch affixed to the upper right arm of his uniform. That symbol has always made me feel uncomfortable. I don't know why. I think it's the sharp edges of those five arms, spiraling out of the central pentagon with a kind of crude authoritarianism.

"Quarantine the diseased Chin!" someone in the crowd yells. "He doesn't belong here!"

The Chin man hangs his head in defeat as he's led away by two men with SAFE emblazoned in capital orange letters on their vests. The Constantinans roar with approval. There's nothing I can do. As the representative of the Governor on election day, Paul's authority on this supersedes mine.

"Good riddance," Paul yells, egging them on from the balcony of the Governor's summer residence as he smiles broadly through his blue-tinged syntho mask. "What a loser. Let's hear it for our SAFE agents, who work hard to protect us from the aliens. Now that it's just us of Europan blood, here's some awesome news. You're all going to get extra money to help you through the pandemic!"

I've had enough. I turn away from the now rapturously cheering crowd as I hear Paul continue to spew his inane propaganda.

"I'm not supposed to be telling you this," he announces with childish excitement, "but I'm sure you can keep a secret. We're working on improving testing for the Chin virus, so we can tell who's infected. I mean, we already can, of course. We'll just do it better. Didn't I tell you I'd take care of you?"

I'm glad to be out of hearing range as I hurry along the road. Looking around me, I see garish mansions, out of place in the backdrop of the ancient mountains just across the Shenandoa. Nowadays, I too feel out of place in this part of town. It seems artificial and foreign to me. At least they kept the old cobblestone streets. I grip my walking stick more firmly to rush away quickly. Behind me I hear the tapping of a woman's heels on the stone. I know she's approaching me because I can smell her floral perfume. I try to accelerate my pace, but she catches up with me. When she speaks, her voice is near.

"Don't you lead the agency of SAFE?"

Out of politeness I stop and turn. I've seen her once before. Her name is Beatrice Holden. She works closely with the President. The syntho mask covers her entire head, just as mine does. Yet her attractiveness shines through the plastic.

"How did that Chin get in here?" she asks.

She's standing very close to me, closer than any woman other than my mother and grandmother have stood.

I suddenly feel clammy and awkward. Her provocatively tight pants and blouse trigger an unfamiliar sensation in my loins. I am stunned into silence for several seconds by her captivating green eyes and wavy brown hair.

"We don't yet restrict the movement of people within our land," I manage to finally say.

"Well, we should," she shoots back, staring with unabashed directness into my eyes.

Then, furrowing her brow, she removes the mask and tosses it carelessly onto the street.

My eyes follow her movement. "It would be better if you didn't throw the mask away like that."

"Why?" she asks carelessly, shaking her head to air her tresses.

I can hardly breathe as I take in the light reflecting off of her disarmingly beautiful irises. "We have a shortage of personal protective equipment."

"We'll manage," she says, unperturbed, now beginning to take off her thick syntho gloves.

It's difficult for me to kneel because of my leg. I certainly don't like to attempt it in front of others. But I can't let her litter my town with syntho. They're bad enough for the environment even when disposed of properly. Fortunately, I've mastered the art of picking things up off of the ground with my walking stick. I balance myself on both feet, taking my weight off of the stick for just a few moments. Long enough to maneuver the end of the stick to swoop in under the mask and gloves and pull them toward me. As soon as the syntho is in my hand, I find my stability again by leaning on the stick. Her gaze follows the movement of my hand as I stuff her discarded personal protective equipment into one of the large front pockets of my well-worn suit jacket.

She stops and watches me, but doesn't move to help. "Why were you defending that Chin?" she asks.

I'm surprised by her question but try to respond as gently as possible.

"He has the right to move about the country, just as we do."

"If that's true, it isn't right," she says.

As attractive as I find her physically, her words and her gestures repel me. Not wanting to prolong this encounter, I begin moving away, but Beatrice follows me.

"Aliens have no business being where we live," she says, a jarring viciousness coloring her tone. "They should know their place."

"And whom do you define as an alien?"

She laughs mirthlessly. "You're funny. Everyone who's not Europan, of course."

I continue walking without looking at her. "We wouldn't be here without aliens, as you call them. They helped us build this town."

"Nonsense," she snorts. "How could they be helpful with anything? They're meant to follow orders and that's all. Sometimes they can't even do that properly."

I grip my walking stick so tightly that my knuckles become even more pale. In vain I try to prevent my left leg from dragging across the cobblestones. Consciously pushing away my frustration, I remind myself that these opinions have been fed to Constantinans since birth. I also remember that the moment people feel insulted, it is much easier for them to stop listening.

"They helped us heal our sick and dying," I say with as much patience as I can muster. "They deserve our respect and gratitude."

This is the town of my birth, of my childhood, of my entire life. My forefather was tasked with establishing a frontier settlement on the southeastern bank of the winding Shenandoa River. Only wilderness existed here a few hundred years ago. My mother raised me on the stories that the elders of this town have been telling since its establishment. The Europan settlers relied heavily on the advice, materials, and help that the natives gave us so generously. Our ancestors would have perished here on the westernmost boundary of Constantina had the people here, none of them of Europan descent, not shown us such kindness. I would have died as a child, had one of their healers not tended to me with compassion.

"You must be delusional," the woman strolling beside me sputters. "The only thing they're good for is cheap labor. They deserve nothing."

I've been walking as briskly as I am able, and despite her high heels, she's been keeping up without effort. We've entered the oldest quarter of Cardiff. The houses here are very different from the newfangled multi-storied brick-and-mortar houses in the wealthy quarter. A sturdy one-storied adobe construction was what my forefather had decided to implement. I can't help but feel a great sense of pride at the hard work and simplicity of my ancestors. This feeling ebbs, however, when I notice the woman looking around with distaste.

"Run-down houses like these are probably where aliens live," she comments, "like rats in an infested hole."

I speak to women only very seldom. When I'm obliged to do so, I find it challenging to look into their faces. But with this woman it's especially difficult. I don't quite know why. She awakens so many unfamiliar emotions within me. My mother's voice rings in my ears.

"Fear of rejection being one of them," it says.

Suddenly I find myself having a conversation in my head with my mother. I'm quite certain that this is how a real back-and-forth would proceed, since I know my mother's perspective on life and on me better than I know anyone else's.

"Mother, why do you always reproach me?"

"I rebuke you, my dear son, because you underestimate yourself."

"I don't, Mother. Look at me. Why would any woman want me?"

"I am looking at you, my one and only precious child. You are a miracle that God gave to your father and me."

"Yes, I know that you had given up on having children. And then I came along."

"No, silly boy, that's not it at all. From the time you were a baby, you shone with a compassion so warm that people from all across Cardiff flocked to you."

"Old people, Mother. Old people flocked to me."

"So what's wrong with old people?" Mother asks, feigning offense.

"Nothing, Mother," I chuckle. "But it would have been nice for a young woman to flock to me once in a while too."

"Never hand over your happiness to another, Buni," she cautions, using the nickname that only my mother ever uses.

"But I've observed the happiness that you and Father shared for most of your lives. That's what I wish to feel."

"I'll say it again, Buni. Don't hand over your happiness to anyone else. It's your most precious possession, the ability to love yourself as you are."

Mother's voice recedes into the innermost spaces of my mind. I inhale deeply and gaze fondly at the old houses around me.

"This is the oldest quarter," I note as I continue walking, my eyes fixed upon the narrow cobblestone road. "This is where my ancestors first established this town."

Beatrice suddenly overtakes me so that I have no choice but to look at her.

"Wait!" she exclaims.

A feeling of dread begins to spread through me.

"Surely, you can't be telling me that you live here among these poor people?"

## BANISHMENT

*You mock me yet again, time, catapulting me without warning from past to present. From the cobblestone streets of Cardiff to this sterile room inside the Governor's Mansion in the capital, Robinson. My essence no longer mistakes itself to be that of Bunim. I am Maya once more.*

*Before this moment, I had never had occasion to even talk to Bunim, let alone feel him from within. Indeed, his mother was right. He does shine with the light of compassion. How delicate his sentiments. How gentle his sensitivities. He was genuinely dismayed as the Chin man was arrested and escorted away by his own agents. As I look across the table at this affable man, I observe his face noticeably relaxing.*

*His agitation has subsided, and my mind releases its hold on that of Bunim.*

*Instead, disquiet has swollen within the young woman sitting next to me. The gravity of this moment weighs on even this most amiable of beings: innocent, compassionate Xetal. I am ashamed to admit that at times I envy the sheltered life she has led. I cannot help but wonder how filled with love she would be had she experienced as much hardship as I have. In this moment, however, her memories are pouring despair into her heart. Her uncharacteristic unease draws me in against my will. Her thoughts dwell on that same day in the past, when the poor Chin man was led away by SAFE. She is remembering that summer solstice four years ago. Far away from Cardiff, in the dark of night. It was her first encounter with the Constantinans as she stood hidden within a forest along the western shore of the Chesapeake Peninsula.*

*I am fighting — trying to resist being pulled into her thoughts, into the clutches of the past. But to no avail. My essence is transforming into hers, drawn in by her grief.*

*Xetal, I apologize for invading your mind and your body. I cannot control myself.*

*I am Xetal, concealed among ancient trees lining the Wicomico Cove.*

Why have people from the land of the settlers across the Chesapeake Bay arrived at our shore? They are forbidden from crossing the waters. Yet they have docked a large boat on the northern bank of the cove, and hundreds of men, women, and children are being forced to walk down its wide wooden ramp. Are those men, with what appear like turtle shells on their heads, beating the people with sticks? The moonlight reflects off their clothes, and I see the letters SAFE.

A young woman with shiny black hair and a face not unlike mine shields herself from the blow of a stick made of a strange material the color of rain clouds.

"How dare you beat me and order me out of my town!" she cries. "Do you have any idea who I am? Get your syntho stick away from me!"

A somewhat older, pale man approaches the tall man who is beating the woman. The older man's head and hands are engulfed in the same syntho material as the beating stick. But the material is like water. Light passes through it, revealing a troubled face with a broad mustache underneath large eyes. The man is in pain. I feel it. It is not just because of his weakened left leg and his limp right wrist. The pain flows from something else, something buried within. I wish to help him. But first I must know what ails him. My grandmother, the Elder Healer of my people, taught me how to read the mist surrounding and pervading all that lives.

"When there is balance, water flows freely, my child," Grandmother used to say. "But when there is imbalance, water hesitates."

She taught me how to discern the flow of water within and without life so that I could help restore balance and health. I breathe in deeply and focus all of my senses on the man. He was gripped with polio in his childhood. And with loneliness.

"Stop!" the man shouts, leaning on a wooden walking stick. "It's bad enough that we're forcing these people to leave behind their homes."

The tall man with SAFE glowing on his chest stops beating the woman and addresses the older man. "But they're Chin, Sir. They're the ones who caused this virus pandemic."

"How absurd!" the young woman shouts. She pushes away the man holding the beating stick, then speaks directly to the older man. "I am Doctor Qingshan Han, one of the most prominent scientists of our time. I order you to release me now!"

The older man's sad, amber eyes glisten in the moonlight. "This is for your own protection and that of others, Doctor Han," he assures her. "It's the job of my SAFE agents to keep you and everyone else safe."

The woman called Qingshan coughs. The mist around her is burdened. The water droplets emanating from her lungs are heavy with what is weakening her. Grandmother taught me how to taste the song of water. If we are still enough to listen, water sings of what it holds. I calm my mind by closing my eyes. Even though I am quite a distance away, I can taste the mood of the waters outside of her. The droplets are heavy and disconsolate.

This Chin woman, as the pale men say she is called, is infected with a virus. I have sensed viruses before among our people. But none that understands the nature of water as well as this one. Water appears to be the chosen element of this being. The virus thrives in water and uses it to spread.

Suddenly, a desperate young Chin man approaches the man who withstood polio. The mist about him sings to me that this young man, too, is burdened with the virus. His body is weak with disease and worry.

"What have you done with my sick wife and my two young children?" he implores. "I cannot find them."

The older man turns to the tall SAFE agent and asks, "Where is this man's family?"

"Sir," the other responds without hesitation, "the President ordered the sick to be taken to the death camps."

The knuckles on the man's left hand become drained of blood as he grips his walking stick more tightly. The mist around him is heavy with sadness.

"I'm sorry," he says to the young Chin man. "I really am. But there's nothing I can do. No one can leave the camps until they recover. Those are the President's orders."

"Then take me to the death camps too," the man pleads. "I cannot forsake my family in such a time."

A short SAFE agent standing nearby quietly addresses the man with the walking stick.

"There isn't a prohibition against people voluntarily entering those camps, is there, Sir?"

"No," the older man says, "but we would have to obtain permission from the President."

"And how long would that take?" the short SAFE agent asks.

"Several months," says the other SAFE agent who had been beating the Chin woman.

The older man vigorously massages his weakened right wrist with his left hand. The short SAFE agent steps closer to him. Even from here, I can hear the concern in his hushed voice. "Isn't there something else we can do?"

The tall SAFE agent becomes incensed in an instant. "How dare you suggest breaking protocol!" he shouts.

"Men, stop," the mustached man orders. He shakes his head sadly and turns to look at the Chin man. "We cannot take you, Sir. I am truly sorry."

The young man falls to his knees. Grief flows in sorrowful waves out of his body to merge with the still waters of the Chesapeake Bay mere steps away from him to the west. The men of SAFE have forced all of the Chin people onto the narrow sandy shore. No one is left on the big boat docked on the northern side of the cove. Beyond the sand in the east lies the ancient forest, hiding me. This thick silence of the night is unfamiliar. Perhaps she is wary of instilling any more fear in these unfortunate Chin. If it were not for the moonlight enveloping the cove, I would not see several of the SAFE men retreating to the boat.

The man with the walking stick begins to bend down to console the distressed young Chin man. But immediately, two men of SAFE hurry up to the older man and grab him with their syntho gloved hands. They begin leading him back to the boat in the distance, even though he resists. I sense that he does not wish to leave the Chin. The SAFE agents remaining on the shore follow quickly. The Chin men and women are too confused to discern what is happening, until one of them speaks out.

"Where do you think you're all going?" the one called Qingshan yells. "I demand that you take me back with you."

The young man who enquired about his family remains where he fell to the ground, just a few paces away from my hiding place. He is surrounded by a few who console him. But as the Chin begin to realize that they are about to be left behind, many of them run frantically in the direction of the boat, in pursuit of the men of SAFE. Four SAFE agents form a protective layer around the man with the walking stick. Other SAFE men beat back the advancing Chin people with their sticks. The mustached man shouts at his men to stop, but they ignore his orders, and he is rushed up the ramp onto the boat.

One of the SAFE men threatens the crowd, the ramp a few steps behind him. "Stand down, or we will take you to the death camps to die with the rest of your kind!"

"Yes!" the young Chin man cries, jumping up from where he had collapsed. "Take me with you to the death camps."

A second man, the only other SAFE agent not on the boat, talks into the ear of the first agent, who yells at the young man again.

"You misheard me, Chin," he lies. "I said that we'll dump you into the Chesapeake Bay if your people don't stand down."

The two SAFE men scramble up the ramp, which is then hurriedly retracted onto the deck. Five Chin men throw themselves against the side of the boat. One of them latches on to the railing. But a SAFE agent pries his fingers loose and the Chin man falls into the water, along with the other four. Even though the boat is far away from the trunk of the ancient oak tree that hides me from everyone's view, I can see an expression of horror contort the older man's face. The SAFE men holding him tighten their grip on his arms as the anchor is hauled up. Slowly the large boat detaches itself from the shore of the cove and flows away on the salty waters of the Bay, leaving behind hundreds of Chin men, women, and children.

As night swallows the boat on the western horizon, groups of Chin huddle together on the narrow strip of sand. Children cry and cling to their parents. A few men shout in frustrated anger. Most of the women and the elderly ponder in silence. Closest to where I am hiding stands the one called Qingshan. At first she is by herself, but soon she is joined by a man, an old woman, and a boy about twelve years old.

"Do you know where they've brought us?" the man asks.

"To the Chesapeake Peninsula, across the Bay from Constantina," Qingshan responds with annoyance.

"We heard you telling that pale man that you are a prominent scientist," the old woman says, ignoring the younger woman's rudeness. She is peering into the forest that I hope still conceals me. "We thought that perhaps you'd know something."

"I don't know any more than you do," Qingshan snaps.

The man admonishes the old woman, "Mother, she doesn't wish to be bothered."

Undeterred, the old woman asks Qingshan, "What kind of scientist are you?"

"Why does it matter?" Qingshan snaps.

"Grandmother," the boy interjects fearfully, pulling on the old woman's sleeve, "what if the primitives devour us?"

"Don't talk nonsense, child," the old woman scolds him. "The people native to this land do not devour others."

"You don't know that with certainty, Mother," the man mumbles.

"Ever since the pandemic began, Father has been telling sister and me that the pale men will chase us away from their cities and towns because it's our fault," the boy says, still tugging on his grandmother's dress.

"Your father is an ignorant peasant!" Qingshan snarls. "This pandemic is not our fault."

The man's face becomes distorted in burgeoning anger. He advances toward Qingshan and opens his mouth. But before he can say anything, the old woman squeezes between them.

"Almost all of us are infected with the virus," she says. "If we are to survive here in this place that appears untouched by humans, each of us needs to contribute our most useful skill."

Qingshan's agitation grows. "Can't you see?" she wails. "They've abandoned us in the wilderness to fend for ourselves against the primitives and the animals."

The old woman remains composed as she tries to soothe Qingshan.

"Doctor Han, my name is Mei. I am a nurse. My son, Ling, is a carpenter. What type of scientist are you?"

"I specialize in ethnobotany," Qingshan replies as she begins to calm down.

"Then you can help prepare medicines from the plants in that forest," the old woman says, pointing in my direction.

"Where's your family?" the boy asks suddenly, staring at the younger woman.

Qingshan's lower lip begins to quiver. For several moments she is unable to speak.

"I don't know," she finally blurts out. "SAFE has been very successful in its effort to break us apart, hasn't it? Separate family and community members from each other before packing us into trucks and boats headed in different directions."

The man looks at her. "My wife and daughter were separated from us too," he says flatly. Then he turns to the old woman. "There must be other carpenters here, Mother. I'll find them and we'll begin building shelter."

"Can you not wait until dawn, my son?"

The man looks up at the cloudless black sky. "There are still many hours of night left. We must work quickly in case the rains decide to come."

Gazing up at the darkness, the old woman nods her head.

"If I can gather fifteen more men, we can build a temporary structure large enough to hold all of us," the man declares as he begins walking away. "If we begin working now, by tomorrow night we can all sleep protected from the animals and the primitives."

"You shouldn't speak this way about the native people," the old woman says, but her son is already too far away to hear her.

The old woman looks again in the direction of the forest. Can she sense my presence somehow? She sighs and turns her gaze on the younger woman.

"Let's find out what other types of scientists are here with us so that together you can find a way to stop this virus."

"Without a laboratory?" Qingshan asks.

"Yes, Doctor Han," the old woman says with a smile. "Scientific discovery in the lap of nature, just like we did it for thousands of years in the Chin homeland we left to come to Constantina."

*Suddenly, my essence separates from that of Xetal. I am Maya once more. How surly you are, time, ejecting me so jarringly from the past into the present. I am a mere puppet on your fingers. Tell me, do you enjoy my discomfort? Does it amuse you to drag me from point to point in the web of Cause and Effect and observe my bewilderment? Why have you singled me out, time? Are you so lonely that you desire my company?*

*I look around the table. Those very individuals who were responsible for the torture and deaths of so many innocent people are seated here. I shudder at Xetal's recollection of that moonlit night when Bunim led his SAFE agents to banish the Chin from Constantina. Her remembered anxiety entices me once more. I cannot escape her memories. Their sinewy fingers reach for me.*

*I again helplessly transform into Xetal as she was that night when the Chin were abandoned in the wilderness.*

The pale people are well aware that all of the Chesapeake Peninsula, east of Constantina and of the Chesapeake Bay, are the ancestral lands of our peoples. It does not matter whether they call us primitives or natives. They know that it is we who inhabit this cove and the forests and rivers beyond it. The boat carrying the men of SAFE has left without the Chin people it brought here. The pale people have exiled their sick and are dumping them on our ancestral lands. The mist that hovers around the Chin brims with disease. If the sick stay here, they shall alter the balance of Mother Earth.

I cannot stay concealed among the trees watching these unfortunate people. I must return to the village. The trees sense my agitation as I walk briskly along the bank of the river that flows from farther north to this cove.

"They bring disease," the misty breath of an ancient maple tree sings to me.

"I know, Mother," I reply, exhaling my thoughts into the mist. "They are afflicted by a virus."

"The disease I speak of is not of the body, but of the mind."

"I do not understand."

"They have forgotten that our roots are all connected to each other."

"Yes, Mother. But what can I do?"

"You must help them, for otherwise all shall perish."

I convey my thoughts of gratitude to the ancient maple tree and resume walking up the riverbank. Soon I glimpse the canoe that brought me here. What a sturdy canoe it is, crafted beautifully from the bark of an old poplar tree by the hands of Mother Nuna's brother. The gentle waters of the river have kept it company. I must travel upstream toward the village of Mother Nuna. The ancient maple tree speaks the truth. All life is in danger. I must warn our people.

# CHAPTER THREE

# MYSTERIES OF DEATH

## ORIGIN

*Time, you have pulled me out of the past with great haste. Once more I am in the present and inhabit my own mind and body. Even though only Xetal, Bunim, and Qingshan experienced that night when the Chin were exiled, everyone seated at this table also knows what occurred. Yet none of them speaks of those atrocities. None takes responsibility for what was perpetrated. I look across the table to those seated there. They are unable to look me in the eye. Out of shame? Or out of arrogance? I wonder.*

*Xetal's mind is still imprisoned in the past, the anxiety she suffered almost suffocating her. Helplessly my mind embraces hers and I am catapulted into a time nine months after the Chin exile. I apologize once more, Xetal, for resonating with your mind without your permission. But your remembered despair begs me not to forsake it. My essence is transforming into that of Xetal.*

*I am no longer Maya. I am Xetal, walking toward a person who is alien to this land.*

How peculiar to be walking here along this riverbank that now no longer is free. Never before have I spoken to the foreigners that inhabit the land they now call Constantina. Never have I visited any of their settlements. I can see hundreds of closely spaced dwellings just beyond the swell of the small hill ahead. How peculiar that I see no trees in their settlement, only large buildings protruding out of the earth they have covered with stones.

As the woman approaches, I see that she is pale, with wavy brown hair and green eyes. She speaks to me with annoyance.

"I'm Beatrice," she announces. "The President told me to meet you here in Cardiff. Why do you need to see where the pandemic began?"

She is not at peace. The unrest within her is palpable. What causes her to be so angry? What causes her to be so unhappy? The mist around this woman called Beatrice is burdened. But not in the same manner as what I tasted around the Chin.

"The President has asked for the help of my people," I offer quietly, looking into her eyes.

She snorts, an ugly sound. "Help? From you primitives? What could you possibly help us with?"

"The President has asked us to help you fight the pandemic."

Beatrice stares at me, stupefied. "The pandemic? Why on earth would anyone ask for your help with a medical issue? We have it completely under control."

"Is it not true that thousands of people are still dying every day?" I ask calmly.

Beatrice looks aghast. "No! Of course not."

I observe her compassionately. "Is everyone who has been infected with the virus receiving care?"

"What? Of course they are."

"How many people live in this settlement you call Cardiff?"

"I don't know. Ten thousand probably. Pretty normal for a frontier town of this size."

"Ten thousand people!" I exclaim. "Crowded into such a small space?"

I reach out to touch her wrist. The moment my skin touches hers, I know.

"The virus has infected you," I say gently.

She yanks her arm away in anger. "Nonsense. You don't know what you're talking about. I don't have any symptoms. The doctor didn't even think it was necessary to have me tested."

I breathe deeply to steady myself. "Perhaps you should be tested."

"Look," Beatrice snaps, "just do what you came here to do. Look around in the place the Chin virus originated and be done with it. So you can go back to the wilderness that spawned you."

I wander away from her. I am drawn to the river, the one our people named Shenandoa thousands of years ago. The cloudless blue sky is reflected in its ripples. I kneel on the riverbank next to the reeds and dip the tips of my fingers into the water. I close my eyes to remember Grandmother's words from many years ago.

"Listen to the rivers," she would tell me in her soft voice aged with wisdom, "for the rivers have nourished life long before humans were even a seed within the womb of Mother Earth."

I hold my breath and listen. I listen with my left hand immersed in the water. I listen with my heart. And soon the river tells me what she has witnessed. Her sadness gushes into me.

"The virus did not originate here," I mumble. "It flowed from upstream."

I look up at the perfectly uninterrupted blue above. Rising to my feet, I walk back toward the other woman and repeat my findings, more audibly this time. She glares at me and snorts once more. But the venom in her being becomes stuck in her throat. She begins coughing just as I approach her.

When she finally stops, she crosses her arms and glares at me. "How could you possibly know that the virus didn't start here?" she demands.

The water droplets in her cough hover in the air before me. I taste the virus within them. It is too late for me to move away. I know that it has seeped into me.

"You should not be around others," I say to her calmly. "You are transmitting the virus."

The flow of water in my body has changed, creating dissonance within me. I can sense the dissonance growing, spreading through my body, and extending to my mind. I close my eyes in an attempt to restore equilibrium. As I focus my mind on the blood moving through my arteries, I hear a distant rumbling above. I concentrate more intently on the cells in my lungs. Raindrops trickle into my hair.

I barely notice Beatrice walking away from me.

"How dare you tell me what I should or shouldn't do!" she calls over her shoulder. "Who the demon do you think you are? Find your own way around."

I direct all of my energy inward, focusing fiercely on the movement of the virus within me. The drizzle of water from the sky transforms into a torrent. I taste the virus rejoicing within my body. It is multiplying quickly. I am unable to control the waters within and so the tumult is manifesting itself above and around me. I taste the power the virus has over the streams in my body. My life shall ebb into nothingness if I cannot vanquish this intruder.

The river sings loudly so I can hear her over the upheaval within me.

"You must seek the source of the virus," her melody instructs me.

In the sudden storm that I have unwittingly caused, my poplar canoe has become adrift. I raise my left arm to rearrange the waters around it so that it comes to a halt on the bank near me. I step into the canoe and seat myself on one of the wooden planks. As I plunge my left hand into the river, waves form behind the canoe, propelling it upstream at great speed.

Despite sheets of rain obscuring my view of the mountains to the west of the Shenandoa, I taste the mist in the air becoming more and more sluggish. The gentle mountain slopes yield to steep cliffs that appear to extend all the way into the dark clouds above. Only a narrow strip of earth separates the river from the stark rock rising from the ground on my left. Within moments, my canoe approaches the entrance of a cave near the shoreline. I can barely see the square opening in the cliff, about two people tall and equally wide. The air here is laden with water that is especially pungent. I recollect through the fog in my mind that I have tasted such acrid mist before. But where?

Suddenly, my chest heaves. I am unable to breathe.

"Mother Shenandoa!" I gasp, grabbing my chest with my left hand and standing up abruptly.

I reach out to the river through the rain pounding on my sinuses. The canoe capsizes and I fall into the river. Before I can hold onto the poplar craft that Mother Nuna had so kindly lent me for this journey, it drifts away in the current. I am given no time to grieve the loss, for my lungs are so heavy that they cause me to sink into the tumultuous waters. My body aches in every joint and bone and muscle. I am too weak to save myself.

Suddenly, I hear Mother Shenandoa singing to me. "Steady yourself, my child. Calm the waters within you. Do not allow fear to conquer you."

I still my mind. I will my thoughts to climb out of the well of panic in which they are drowning. I concentrate and suffuse my body with strength so that I can resurface and swim the short distance to the shore. There I lie, relaxing my lungs. Within a few moments, I am able to inhale and then exhale. Inhale and exhale again. I breathe slowly, focusing my mind away from the pain coursing through my body.

"Why has this virus affected me so?" I convey my thoughts to the river through the mist emanating from me.

"This being flourishes in water. Just as you do."

"I do not understand, Mother."

"Of the five elements, it is water from which you draw your special abilities, Xetal," the Shenandoa sings. "You wield great power because water flows almost unobstructed through you."

"Does water not flow through others as freely?"

"No, my child. Those with diseased minds impede the flow of water and of all the elements within them, creating imbalance."

"Is this why the virus has not been able to defeat Beatrice?"

"My child, you must preserve your strength. Close your eyes and focus your attention inward."

I focus on my breath. That pungent smell again. What does it remind me of? Once when I was four years old, I ventured into a small cave near my ancestral village, far from here. I remember wetness, almost as though I was standing under a waterfall. Suddenly, as I wandered through the darkness, a pair of small, round eyes pierced into mine. Grandmother had always taught me to be brave. And so quietly I walked toward the eyes. They belonged to a furry face attached to a pair of folded wings. It was my first encounter with a bat, hanging upside down, sleeping. Until I had disturbed his slumber.

It is that same smell that wafts out onto the cliffs here.

"Bats!" I exclaim into the mist. "They must live in that cave."

"No longer," Mother Shenandoa sings mournfully. "The pale humans chased them away from their sleeping caverns."

"I must go inside."

"Why, my child?"

I do not know why. But something from inside the mountain compels me. I breathe energy into my arms and legs and lift myself up onto my feet. My head spasms and I almost collapse again. I inhale as deeply as I am able and walk unsteadily into the cave. I wander along a rocky corridor that slopes upward and narrows after a short while. As I step deeper into the cave, darkness engulfs me. Only the dim glint of a few nearby calcium deposits dripping from the ceiling are visible to me now. When I feel myself stumbling on the uneven ground, I press my palms against the damp walls and keep moving. Onward and upward. Why, I do not know. Something beckons me. I must not stop.

My body grows weaker and weaker as the virus swims unencumbered through the currents of my blood. My lungs are drowning. But I cannot stop. So every few steps I focus my mind and reinvigorate my body. These spurts of energy enable me to climb deeper into the mountain's abdomen. I do not know how much time passes by. My mind is so perturbed that I cannot sense what lies ahead of me. I sense only that the virus that now flourishes within me used to live in the bats that called this place their home. The pale men must have destroyed their habitat. For otherwise they would be here.

I feel my life flowing out of my body. The virus now commands the waters within my organs. Within moments, my legs shall no longer be strong enough to support my weight. At least the cave floor has become level. It no longer slopes upward, but the corridor has widened significantly. Something has changed. I sense a reverberation within the hollow of this mountain. The remembered smells of that cave from my childhood mingle with those of the present. My eyes have adjusted to the darkness. I see the outline of a rivulet meandering around the shadowy stalagmites rising from the rocky ground near my moccasined feet. The creek seems determined to reach some destination. Where? Dampness, dankness, wetness. Water everywhere. Outside of me. Within me. The massive weight of it crushing me from all sides.

I extend my left foot to take a step, expecting to collapse onto the hard rock of the cave floor. But I have reached the edge of a cliff within the bowels of the mountain. As I fall along with the waters of the rivulet into the abyss below, my breath stops. Let me not yield to fear of death. Let my thoughts instead dwell on Mother.

## REVIVAL

*As Xetal begins to lose consciousness, my own essence as Maya separates sufficiently from hers for me both to know Xetal's inner experience and to observe her as Maya.*

*Suddenly the painful squeezing of Xetal's organs vanishes as her consciousness fades and she falls freely into the abyss. Life ebbs away from Xetal's body. For the briefest of moments, I, Maya, experience Xetal dying. But once more I am not to find peace in the lap of death. My essence severs itself completely from hers. I transform yet again. Not into someone else, but into myself of the present.*

*Secure in my own body and mind as Maya, I look around, at the faces of the twelve men and women seated with me at this long table inside the Circular Office in the Governor's Mansion. I remember having traveled to Cardiff that day, when I learned that Xetal was going to be sent there by the President. When I didn't find her in the frontier settlement and suddenly torrents of rain erupted from the clear blue sky, I communed with the winds. They whispered to me to rush to the sleeping caverns of the bats. I saw Xetal enter the cave, just as the rains began to subside. Hurriedly, I ran after her into the dank darkness.*

*Time, you sweep my mind away to that day three and a half years ago.*

*I am Maya of my past.*

I stand inside the hollow of the mountain, at the edge of the cliff, beyond which the meandering rivulet has hurled itself. As I peer through the shadows before me, I discern Xetal's falling form in the abyss below. I see the virus within each crevice of her dying body as she sinks farther into the blackness. I raise my right hand, palm-side up. I gaze intently at the air just above my fingers until a small eddy of it begins to form and spiral in place above my outstretched hand. The eddy gathers force and grows in size into a swirling vortex of air. I close my eyes, feeling the eagerness of the vortex swelling above my palm. Then I redirect my focus to the air through which Xetal is plunging.

I can sense the vortex blow with great alacrity from my palm into the abyss, overtaking Xetal's body. Her fall slows as currents of air form a cushion below her. My mind is unwavering. My thoughts dwell only on the air below Xetal's body. Soon she floats in the darkness, no longer plunging to her death. I direct my energy to the currents beneath her and direct them upwards.

Slowly I open my eyes and see the vortices of wind I have created around her gently raise her toward the ceiling of the cave. Her body is limp, life hanging on by barely a breath. Soon she floats near my feet above the dark emptiness of the abyss.

I speak softly to the body hovering before me.

"My sister, this virus has exploited your nature and is thriving within you. For the element of the virus is water — the same as yours. I must pull this being out of you. Otherwise, you shall not survive the death that has all but carried you away."

I close my eyes once more and raise both my arms with my palms facing down toward her form drifting before me. I force air into her body floating above the abyss. More and more air. It is the only way I can think of to displace the laden droplets of water within her cells. Nothing happens at first as Xetal begins to swell. I cannot allow doubt to creep into my thoughts. I continue focusing on the arrows of air piercing through her skin. Soon drops of water begin rising out of the pores of Xetal's skin, carrying the virus and its many progeny within them.

Countless droplets seep out from her toward the cavern ceiling, from which moist stalactites large and small drip down. Thousands of miniscule spheres of water rise from Xetal's floating body. Then millions. Each burdened with the virus. They had inundated her organs and blood. I do not stop until the last virus particle has been siphoned out of her.

At long last, I see no virus in the water leaving her skin. And so I cease the onslaught of air on her debilitated body. Instead, I focus once more on the vortex of air holding her up and direct it to glide her body onto the cavern floor near my feet. Just as she is lowered to the rocky ground, Xetal begins to stir.

She opens her eyes and looks at me in confusion. "What happened to me?"

I breathe in deeply and say, "You were infected with the virus."

"I remember," she says weakly, then hesitates for a few moments. "I remember stepping into nothingness. I remember falling."

"Yes."

Supine on her back, her eyes open wide.

"Did you pull me out of the abyss?"

I smile.

"You saved my life, sister," Xetal whispers gratefully as she sits up with some effort. "Who are you?"

"I am Maya," I respond.

I hold out my right hand for her. Hesitantly, she extends her left hand toward me. When our palms touch, vigor from my body flows into hers. Her face becomes suffused with color and surprise.

"You are of our people," she declares with wonder.

I simply smile and pull her up to her feet. "Come. We must leave this cave. You need to breathe in fresh air."

"I feel weak," Xetal says feebly.

I extend both of my hands to her.

"Here, put your hands in mine. I shall flow strength into you."

Readily she places both of her palms on mine. I close my eyes and concentrate on the flow of energy within me and then direct it into her. And so we stand for several moments. I inhale and exhale slowly and deeply so as not to deplete my own vigor. When I can sense that her body has become steady, I gently release her hands.

I open my brown eyes to see hers smiling back into mine. She is a beautiful woman, with the high cheekbones and gracefully elongated eyes of her people. How young she is, I observe somewhat longingly. How fortunate she is not to have lived through the hardships that I have had to endure. I feel the contours of my face harden with the stirrings of animosity toward her.

"Are you unwell, sister?" she asks me, concern evident in her face.

"Why?" I shoot back, my voice sounding the smallest bit abrasive even to myself. "Why do you wish to know?" Then I shake my head. "Do not worry. It must be the stale air in this cave. We must leave."

"I am Xetal," she offers, smiling.

"Yes, I know," I say, smiling back, banishing all antagonistic thoughts about her from my mind. "You answered the President's call on behalf of your people."

The younger woman lowers her head. "I was not able to help, for the virus almost vanquished me. I do not understand the power it had over me, even though Mother Shenandoa explained it."

I begin walking away from the precipice toward the cave entrance, motioning her to follow me. "The virus resonates with water more than it does with any other element," I explain.

"Yes, I sensed that too," Xetal mutters. "That is why I thought that I would be able to tame it, for I resonate with water as well."

"We all underestimated the potency of this virus. It is not your failing that the virus subdued you."

"But if you had not come here, my life would have ended."

"Let us not dwell on that."

We walk on in silence along the dank tunnel leading out of the mountain. We follow the downward slope, careful to avoid bumping into the wondrous calcium deposits dripping from the ceiling and rising from the ground. Suddenly I stop in front of a wall, where ancient carvings shine in the dark. One is a symbol known to all of the ancient peoples of earth: the panchika, a small central circle with five softly curved arms leading into it from the periphery. Several panchika, small and large, are carved into the rock. It is as though they are glowing. But how? I take a step closer so that my nose almost touches the indentations in the rocky surface.

"Bioluminescence!" I exclaim.

"Yes," Xetal says, putting her face close to mine to gaze upon the cave wall. "The ancestors of the people of the Shenandoa valley used to coat their cave carvings with specific types of bacteria that glow in the dark."

"Do you know why?"

"I believe they did so to light the cave walls, while reminding people of the importance of what these symbols represent."

I feel the urge to trace my finger along the ancient carvings. But I do not wish to disturb the bacterial paint that has endured for thousands of years. Over a million generations of bacteria have made these carved indentations in the cave rock their home in the past several millennia. Wondrous indeed.

"How ingenious," I declare and smile at Xetal.

We resume our journey out of the cave in companionable silence. When we step out into the open, it takes a few moments to adjust to the brightness of the day. The sky is a cloudless, spotless blue once more. The small dinghy that I arrived in is resting on the riverbank. It is a simple craft, made of wood and painted white, able to comfortably fit only two people. We walk over to it.

"We must journey back to Cardiff," I say grimly.

"Why?" Xetal asks.

"We must find out what the Constantinans are doing."

"You speak of the virus?"

"The settlers are unable to contain the pandemic," I say as I push the boat into the water and hold it steady for Xetal to step inside. "It has been a year and a half."

When we are both seated inside the dinghy, Xetal dips her left hand into the waters and propels us rapidly downstream.

"That is why the President asked for our people's help," she says. "They wish for us to eliminate the virus, for they are unable to do so on their own."

I breathe in deeply and look around me. On our left the plains extend into the horizon, dotted here and there with less greenery than before the settlers arrived. I gaze to the right, upon the mountains passing by as we rush along the river. They are low with rounded peaks, for they form part of an ancient range that has battled the rains and the winds for almost as long as the earth has been in existence. They are covered densely with verdant forests. How many millions of years did it take for the animals and plants and microbes to adapt to each other so that they could live in harmony in those forests? How long did it take predators and prey, insects and birds, reptiles and amphibians, bacteria and viruses to commune with each other to achieve symbiosis? And these Europans destroyed this delicate balance of life in just a few centuries? I cannot prevent anger from surging within me.

"They have brought this pandemic upon themselves," I say, rubbing my upper left arm vigorously. "They should not have burdened the rivers with their waste. They should not have cut down the trees and eroded the soils. They should not have destroyed the ecosystems that have sustained life since long before humans evolved. It is because the pale men devastated the food sources of the nectar bats that the bats ventured out into the settlements and passed on a virus that would never have infected humans otherwise."

We reach the outskirts of Cardiff, where we pull the boat ashore after stepping onto the bank. We begin walking toward the town.

Xetal's young face is contorted with genuine concern.

"But if we do not help them, this pandemic shall spread to beyond the lands they inhabit. Our people too shall become infected."

*Again, you amuse yourself at my expense, time. You have catapulted me back into the present. To this sterile room stifled with plastic furniture and people suffocating in syntho clothes. I don't need to look behind me to know that along the circular wall are positioned secret service agents. To whom are they loyal? Which faction, I wonder. The President is here, sitting at this table. So, too, the Governor. The native inhabitants of this land have come to the aid of Constantinans many times in the past few centuries. But have they ever acknowledged their help? Have they ever traveled in the direction in which they were guided? What is the point of coming to someone's aid, if he keeps making the same destructive choice over and over again? Have they ever acknowledged the contributions of anyone who didn't look like them?*

*One of the secret service agents stirs ever so slightly. The white symbol printed upon the syntho fabric engulfing his upper right arm screams at me. Every time I see this blatant perversion and misappropriation of the panchika, one of our most meaningful and ancient symbols in use for thousands of years, I feel the air draining out of my lungs. Outrage constricts my chest and I have to close my eyes to contain the ire that threatens to destroy what is around me. I shut out the agent and everyone else in the room and I breathe. At first my breath comes in shallow heaves, but then calmness pervades my body. But this peace does not perfuse my thoughts. For my memories of that day when I first met Xetal beckon me so vehemently that I cannot escape their clutches. The present dissolves yet again into the past, moments after Xetal and I stepped onto the riverbank near Cardiff, after I had found her dying in the cavern.*

*I am Maya of the past.*

Xetal and I are within a few steps of the town of Cardiff. It would not be wise for us to be seen.

"Stay close to me," I advise Xetal. "I shall ensure that no one sees us as we walk through the settlement."

I turn my right palm upward to the sky and focus my gaze above my fingers. Gradually, a small sphere of shimmering air forms above my hand. Soon the shimmer transforms into currents of air circling each other, growing stronger and faster. The miniature zephyrs spin into a small sphere. I breathe deeply and direct my thoughts to the air above my palm.

The shimmering sphere of spiraling eddies grows in size until it engulfs both Xetal and me. To the world around us we are camouflaged. Perhaps if they paid very close attention, they might see the air around us tremble. And so, Xetal and I walk invisible to others into the nouveau-riche quarter of Cardiff. We hurry along the streets until we see Bunim, Paul, and Beatrice standing in the middle of a winding cobblestone road. They are engaged in conversation.

"That is the man who led the group that forced the Chin people into exile," Xetal tells me, pointing to Bunim.

Xetal and I approach the others, hidden from view within our shimmering sphere of air. All three are wearing bluish-tinted syntho face masks and gloves. Paul is talking more loudly than necessary to be heard. He speaks disparagingly to Bunim.

"I just don't get it, Buni," he scoffs. "Why are you always siding with the aliens?"

Bunim bristles. "I've told you not to call me that, Paul."

"Whatever, man," Paul says, sounding bored. "You're avoiding the question. What's wrong with you? You're a senior government official. Your concern should be for Constantina."

"My concern is always for Constantina," Bunim declares firmly. "The Chin and the Afrikans are just as much a part of Constantina as is everyone else."

"Bunim!" Beatrice exclaims, "How can you say that? Surely you don't mean that you value us the same as you value them?"

"By us, I take it you mean people of Europan descent?" Bunim asks dejectedly.

"Whom else would she mean, man?" Paul asks, irritated. "I just don't get you. Didn't one of your ancestors build this town or something? You're an old blood, man. So why do you act like this?"

"Old blood?" Bunim is becoming exasperated. "If Europan blood is old, then what is the blood that courses through the veins of the natives?"

Beatrice rolls her eyes. "Not the primitives again."

"You're out of your mind, man," Paul says. "The natives have nothing to do with Constantina. This is our country. And the aliens need to understand that too. We're the ones who decide whether to let them enter and live here. We can just as readily throw them out."

"Is that what Jeranity teaches you?" Bunim asks.

"Hey, you leave my religion out of this."

"Why? Didn't King Jer teach you to be kind to your neighbors?"

Paul, quite a bit shorter than Bunim, takes a step toward him and tries to look menacing. "Don't talk to me about King Jer, Kunish."

Beatrice moves to position herself between the two men, her back to Bunim. "Now, now, boys," she soothes them. "There's no need to bring religion into this."

Paul shakes his head and steps away. Beatrice turns to smile at Bunim. Even from this distance, I can sense his discomfort at her proximity. He moves away from her. Beatrice doesn't seem to notice, as she is busy trying to get Paul's attention.

"So do you know anything more about the vaccine?" she asks Paul.

"No," he replies disinterestedly. "All I know is that they've begun clinical trials. We should have something soon."

"Of course, we'll get it first, won't we?" Beatrice says, eagerness shining in her face.

"Look, guys," Paul says, "I'm bored. I could use a drink."

"A drink?" Bunim asks. "In the middle of the day?"

"Yeah, what's wrong with that? The Governor said I could use his friend's house. He's a really important guy. Let's go there. His bar is fully stocked. I know because I've been there before with the Governor."

"You go ahead," Bunim says, beginning to walk away. "I have work to do."

In the blink of an eye, Beatrice reaches out and grabs Bunim's right elbow. "Oh, come on now, Bunim. Don't spoil the fun. Let's go see this important man's house. You can relax for a few minutes. It won't kill you."

Bunim freezes and stares at Beatrice's hand on his arm. His breathing becomes labored and, as if in a trance, he follows her. The three begin walking down the street to a stately looking mansion at the end of the cul-de-sac. Xetal and I follow closely, still shielded from view by the shimmering sphere of air that engulfs us. On the wide adobe steps leading up to the mansion, I notice Paul and Beatrice stripping off their syntho masks and gloves and carelessly throwing them onto the street. Littering doesn't appear to bother them. Bunim, however, keeps his protective gear on. Paul opens the massive double doors and leads the others into the house.

I speak quietly to Xetal. "Hold my wrist and I shall help you hear beyond the walls of the house."

I close my eyes and focus on the air around us, beginning with what is nearest to me. As my mind calms itself, I sense the vibrations of each molecule of oxygen and nitrogen and water moving around us. I widen my sphere of sensation outward until I can sense the individual atoms in the outer wall of the mansion, and beyond, inside the building. My breathing steadies as my ears attune themselves to the subtle mechanical vibrations generated from within the house. I open my eyes and relay the sound waves through my skin to Xetal.

"What is inside the house, sister?" Xetal asks me.

I inhale deeply and then exhale a steady stream of air waves that travel through the miniscule cracks in the mansion to the rooms inside. I close my eyes and shut out all extraneous sensory input apart from the waves rebounding off of the different surfaces, materials, objects, and people within. The waves reflected back to me coalesce into a visual image, which I then convey to Xetal through my skin.

Beyond the double doors, at the entrance, is a narrow foyer, which opens up into a grand room with exposed wooden ceiling beams and wide hardwood floors. On the far end of the room is a fireplace with two armchairs placed in front of it. Along the wall with several large windows opening out onto the street is a long wooden cabinet that is waist high. On the opposite side of the large room, beyond the plush carpeting and cushioned sofa, stands a man. He is tall, muscular, wet, and naked, apart from a short towel draped around his waist. It is into this great room that Paul steps, followed by Beatrice and then Bunim, who closes the entrance doors behind him.

"Who the demon are you?" Paul demands, annoyance dripping from his voice.

"What is that Duskie doing here?" Beatrice mumbles, her tone simultaneously derogatory and aroused. "Doesn't he feel any shame? Standing there with water glistening on his dark chest and clinging to his dense, spongy black hair?"

"I am Kasin," the man says in a voice filled with confident dignity. "I wasn't notified that anyone would be coming here. Give me a few moments to get dressed."

Kasin turns around slowly and disappears down a corridor. We hear the sounds of bare feet walking on a wooden floor and then a door closing.

Paul begins spewing as soon as the man is out of earshot. "What possible right does a Duskie like him think he has to be here? Here, of all places. Here in this house."

"Who is he?" Beatrice enquires breathlessly.

"I haven't met him before," Bunim responds quietly.

Several moments pass in which Bunim takes off his mask and gloves and holds onto them in his left hand. Soon, the determined steps of slippered feet reverberate from inside the corridor. Kasin reappears, this time fully dressed in an asymmetrically cut long-sleeved, button-less shirt and tight-fitting pants that flare at the ankles. His clothes hug his beautifully sculpted physique, and I find my concentration wavering.

"Sister!" Xetal exclaims. "I am no longer receiving any visual image from you."

I inhale sharply and refocus my attention.

"No one can be here except the Governor's representative," we hear Kasin say. His voice is deep. Authoritative.

Paul erupts into outrage. "How dare you tell us what we can and can't do!"

"Paul," Bunim interjects, "we'll leave. It's not a problem."

"No," Paul shouts. "How dare he ask us to leave. You're the director of SAFE. And I'm the Governor's representative. If anyone should take off, it should be him."

The silence that follows is viscous. But soon Paul speaks again.

"You heard me, Duskie. Get out."

Kasin's voice does not lose its calm. "Director, I must ask you and this young woman to leave. This is private property."

Paul fidgets, while Kasin stands firm. Bunim begins putting on his mask and gloves. Beatrice simply stares hungrily at the tall Afrikan man.

"Paul," Bunim interrupts before the smaller man can say anything else, "I'm going."

Soon the front doors of the mansion open and Bunim and Beatrice walk down the steps. Bunim's head and hands are protected by the syntho mask and gloves. But Beatrice's protective gear is lying discarded on the street. As the green-eyed woman turns to the older man, Xetal releases my wrist. We are still hidden from view by the sphere of air swirling around us.

"Aren't the Duskies all in the death camps?" Beatrice asks flippantly. "Where the scientists are testing the vaccines on them?"

"Please stop using the word Duskie, Ms. Holden." Bunim is unable to look at her face, instead gazing at his feet. "It is an odious word."

Beatrice steps closer to Bunim. It is not difficult to see that her proximity causes him significant unease. She smiles coquettishly at him, puffing out her ample bosom. In an urgent effort to escape her, Bunim almost trips as he hurries down the front steps.

Beatrice catches up effortlessly to Bunim as he limps away from the mansion. "Fine, I won't use the word anymore," she says petulantly.

Bunim does not speak as they walk down the cobblestone street with wall-to-wall two- and three-story brick and concrete buildings on both sides. There is no greenery anywhere. No trees or grass, no space between houses even. Xetal and I follow closely behind them, unseen.

"Look," Beatrice says, modulating her voice to sound almost like that of a little girl, "I'm just concerned about Constantina. This pandemic has become a huge burden on so many people. Really. I just want it to get better."

Bunim stops and turns to look at her. "We are all concerned about the pandemic, Ms. Holden."

Beatrice maneuvers herself around Bunim's walking stick and steps into the empty space in front of him, her face very close to his.

"Call me Beatrice," she coos, touching the collar of his shirt.

As blood rushes into Bunim's cheeks and his body goes quite rigid, I feel pity for him. Beatrice's skin-tight clothes and ample perfume must certainly be very difficult to endure for a man who appears to not have much experience with women. Bunim clears his throat and adjusts his walking stick.

"You know," Beatrice murmurs, pulling his collar toward her, "I'm famished. Why don't you and I go someplace quiet and grab a bite to eat?"

I grab Xetal's hand and lead her quickly away from Bunim and Beatrice. In silence we walk through the streets of Cardiff. I attempt to dissipate the heated annoyance that is rising within me.

"We have the ability to rid them of this disease that is killing so many of them," Xetal says, lost in thought. "We should…"

"Just because we have the power to eliminate the virus does not mean we should," I interrupt.

We have reached the outskirts of the settlement. No Constantinan is in sight. I turn my right palm skyward and focus my thoughts on the air surrounding us. The shimmering sphere hiding us from view transforms into a vortex of winds, which waft into the sky. For a moment, I stare after those winds, envious of their ability to simply drift upward and away. Away from the avarice and stupidity of human beings. Away from the disease and violence that humans cause with their thoughtless actions.

Xetal strolls toward the water. I follow her. For several moments we walk in silence southward along the riverbank, away from the houses and tree-less streets of Cardiff.

"But our people have preserved the health of the rivers and forests for millennia," Xetal laments.

"And in just a few centuries, the settlers have destroyed entire ecosystems," I add, my anger resurfacing.

"But now that they have unleashed a deadly virus upon humanity, should we not stop it?"

Xetal's brown eyes probe mine with so much hope and compassion that I have to look away. A flock of birds flies by and fish frolic in the river. I breathe in several lungfuls of air before turning back to Xetal.

"We are faced with a choice. Do we help them survive or do we allow them to perish?"

## CHAPTER FOUR

# DOUBT IN LOVE

### CHOICE

*Time, you have ejected me from the past into the present once again. My body is still here, seated on this plastic chair at this long plastic table, even as my mind has traveled through many months of time. A strained conversation is taking place among several of those surrounding me. I can hardly discern the words, though, for their emotions are drowning out their speech. Why am I so affected by the pain of others? There are moments when I would much rather avoid their sadness and apprehension. And yet I feel it all, against my will. I become helplessly imprisoned in their grief. If only I could control these unwanted excursions into others. If only I could choose the timing of my empathy. Alas, I cannot.*

*Of all the emotions shouting into my mind, Bunim's are the loudest. I sense a particularly intense disturbance within him. He is overcome with grief over something lost. No, over someone lost. Someone very dear to him. Against my will, his sorrow pulls me in. I apologize, Bunim, for invading your mind. I cannot stop my essence from transforming into yours.*

*I am Bunim of the past, of the day of the vernal equinox two and a half years ago.*

Is the clock on the wall running fast again? Or is it really twenty minutes past six? I'm certain I asked her to come to dinner at six. Did something happen to her? Let me check on the turkey roast. She abhors dry meat, which is why I've been smothering the bird with its own juices every fifteen minutes as it slowly cooks in the oven. Everything must go perfectly today. It simply must. Ah, finally! The doorbell.

Every time I see her, my heart palpitates. She is truly the most ethereally beautiful woman I have had the fortune to be near. There she stands at the threshold of my home, in a crimson dress that flatters her feminine body so well.

"Welcome, Beatrice," I greet her, giving her a warm kiss on the cheek and gesturing for her to come in. "I hope you didn't have any problems finding my home."

"No, not at all," she tells me in her flippantly charming way. "In fact, on my way over here, I decided to step into the new F&L store they opened in the nouveau-riche quarter. I just love that brand. It's so high-end, so chic."

She's late because she was shopping? No, that's no reason to be annoyed. Nor is her calling the river quarter the nouveau-riche quarter a reason to be upset. I must shake off these negative sentiments. I guide her from the small foyer to the small kitchen. Everything in our house is small. This has never bothered me before, but somehow it does now.

"Finally, I get to see the inside of your house, Bunim," she says, then flops down on a wooden chair at the small, circular dining table. "I don't see what the big deal was in you not inviting me to your place these past few months. So it's small. But then everything in the old quarter is small. You can't help it if your ancestors planned it this way."

The smile on my face becomes strained. Beatrice notices.

"You should have seen the orphanage I grew up in," she says quickly, looking at the wall with framed photos of many of my family members, living and dead. "Eight unkempt girls to a small room. Bare walls, paint cracking. Mold everywhere. At least you had a home to call your own when you were a kid."

Whenever she speaks of her desolate childhood, a vehement desire to protect her surges within me. I resist the urge to go over and comfort her, however. For I have learned from experience that she doesn't like demonstrations of what she perceives as pity. Instead, I walk to the refrigerator and ask her if I can get her something to drink. I bought three types of freshly pressed juice, even though fresh food of any kind is very challenging to procure in Constantina.

"I'll just have a soda," she says, her tone indifferent.

"I don't have soda, Beatrice," I mumble. "But I managed to get fresh juice for you. I know how much you love it. I can offer you a selection."

"No," she says, annoyed. "I'm not in the mood for juice today. What's for dinner?"

"Your favorite," I say, my face lighting up at the thought of her enjoying the main course over which I labored for so many hours. "Turkey roast, seasoned just the way you like it."

"Really?" Much to my surprise, Beatrice is not pleased. "You took me out to a turkey dinner two weeks ago. Don't you have anything else?"

I can't suppress the dejection that creeps into my face. Beatrice rises to her feet and places her right hand over my left hand, which is clutching my walking stick tightly.

"It's okay, honey," she teases, kissing me full on the mouth and then nibbling my lower lip. "I'll give your cooking a shot."

She certainly knows how to dissolve my apprehension. Happily, I place my walking stick against the kitchen counter and slide my left hand into an oven mitt. Supporting my weight using my right forearm on the counter, I open the oven door. The extra leverage lets me lift heavier weights with my left hand, while not losing my balance. But it's no easy feat, and it causes me significant pain. Out of the corner of my eye, I see Beatrice looking down at her nails as she returns to her seat at the dining table.

The turkey roast is the centerpiece of the wooden dining table. I've made a salad and some mashed potatoes as well. All are prepared the way Beatrice likes them, even though I care for neither salad nor mashed potatoes.

"You want to know a secret?" Beatrice asks, just before she shovels a spoonful of potatoes into her mouth.

"You shouldn't disclose anything that the President shares with you in confidence, Beatrice," I tell her, repeating advice I have had to give her many times before.

She pouts, which I've learned is a flirtation tactic. "You're no fun, Bunim. Why do you have to be such a killjoy? I'm going to tell you anyway. Listen. So we're going to start sending some of our people to the towns the Afrikans built on Kent Island and the Chesapeake Peninsula."

"Why?" I ask, suddenly having lost my appetite.

"What do you mean, why? Because we need to spread out, of course." As she says this, she continues eating voraciously.

"And by we, you mean us of Europan descent," I mutter, barely able to look at her.

"Of course, I mean us. Who else would I mean? Really, Bunim. I don't know why you keep asking the same old questions. You know that our big cities can't fit all of us anymore. I mean, look at Robinson and Oniosa. They're practically bursting at the seams with Constantinans. And no one lives in Lombardi. It's so antiquated."

"Have the Afrikans been consulted about this plan?" I raise my face to look at her, probing her green eyes with my amber ones.

To my chagrin, she laughs out loud, a hollow, mirthless laugh. "You're really funny sometimes, Bunim. Why should it matter what the Afrikans want?"

I've learned that it's best to keep quiet when Beatrice revels in her bigotry. Logic doesn't work with her in these instances. Something in my face must be revealing my thoughts, because Beatrice changes her tone almost immediately.

"No one cared about what I wanted when I was a child," she says in her little girl voice. "People did whatever they wished and I was forced to go along with it. Some people are just born into bad luck."

"Beatrice," I plead softly, reaching across the table with my fingers to grasp hers.

She looks down at my left hand holding hers and confesses, "Sometimes I feel bad for them. The Chin and the Afrikans and all those other aliens. The natives even. I know what it's like when you don't matter."

"You matter to me, my darling." I can barely utter the words, as tears threaten to choke my voice. "I'm sorry that you were treated so dreadfully. But it's all over now."

Gently she withdraws her hand from mine and wipes her eyes with some measure of violence. "Can we talk about something else, Bunim? I don't like to remember."

I inhale sharply, trying to infuse levity into my voice.

"So how was your day today?"

She gazes deeply into my eyes, gratitude shining brightly for a fleeting moment, before she turns her attention to her plate. She heaps a small mound of mashed potatoes onto her fork and pushes it into her mouth. I can't help but admire the courage with which she faces each day, how she can simply move aside the horrid memories of her loveless childhood and focus on the present.

"Well," she mumbles, her mouth half full of food, "I'm getting bored of Cardiff. I wish the President would send me back to Robinson."

"It's only temporary," I say, trying to hide my disappointment.

Beatrice seems not to have heard me, as she continues speaking. "It's just so plain here, you know? I don't know how you spent your entire life here. You must have been bored out of your mind."

"It's the place of my birth. My family is here. My community is here. Why would I be bored?"

"But there's nothing to do! Except for the few clubs in the nouveau-riche quarter. And those get old real quick."

I don't know how to respond. My appetite has completely disappeared. I try to summon the empathy that filled me just moments ago.

"Beatrice," I say, "you're doing it again."

"What?"

"Belittling my childhood, my life."

She stops chewing and stares at me before saying contritely, "Oh, I wasn't aware."

"I know you don't mean to."

"But everyone is geriatric in this town," she complains. "I can barely turn any heads!"

I shake my head, hardly able to utter the words, "But you and I are together, Beatrice," I point out. "Why do you need to turn heads?"

"I do what I need to so I can survive," she snaps. "I'm not going to apologize for it."

"I don't understand, Beatrice."

"Look, Bunim, different people are born with different gifts. Some can throw a ball real well. Some are great with their minds. I was born with beauty. So why should I let that go to waste?"

"To waste?" I am flabbergasted. "What are you trying to leverage your beauty for?"

Once again, she ignores my words. "What's the difference between someone using their brains for gain and me using my looks?"

I choose to be silent. I've learned that sometimes she just needs someone to listen to her vent. And so that is what I allow her to do. But she is not finished.

"And I just can't stand all the stupid families here!" Beatrice spews.

"Beg your pardon?"

"All those children with their mothers and fathers," she says. "They make me sick."

My voice softens. "I understand, my dear."

"No, you don't," she shouts. "You have no idea. You didn't have to suffer through anything. I did."

I glance over at my walking stick leaning against the table before saying, "Dearest, I..."

"Whenever I see a mother with her child, I feel angry," she interrupts. "Not sad, but angry. Why does that child deserve a parent? Is it special in some way that I'm not?"

I reach across the table to touch her hand again.

"No!" she says, snatching her hand away this time. "You just don't get it! I hate having to walk past yet another display of sickening affection. At least in Robinson, I live in a neighborhood with very few children, so I don't have to be exposed to that."

"I'm sorry, darling," I mutter, feeling helpless at her pain. "I really am."

"I don't care whether you feel sorry or not," she says viciously. "It doesn't change anything. You aren't burdened with my memories. You don't have to constantly suppress the memory of your ninth birthday."

"What happened on your ninth birthday?" I ask with genuine concern.

"You really want to know?" Her tone is belligerent. "I plucked up the nerve to ask the director of the orphanage where my parents were, and do you know what he said? 'Nobody wanted you.' Just like that. No emotion. Then he said, 'So now we're stuck with you.' He had a mustache. Just like you."

I know what's coming next. Not infrequently Beatrice becomes upset at someone else and takes her anger out on me. Well, no one said love was easy. I brace myself for what I know is coming. And sure enough, she explodes. A barrage of recriminations. A recitation of all my faults. Throughout it all I remain silent. Saying anything in my defense will only infuriate her more. I remind myself that I had the good fortune of having a home with parents who loved me, an entire community that adored me. On the other hand, through no fault of her own, she was abandoned as a baby. She had to raise herself in a hostile environment, all the time feeling unloved and unappreciated. She deserves to be loved.

Several minutes go by. She runs out of steam and begins eating voraciously again. Between mouthfuls she tells me about the new clothes she bought from F&L. Soon her plate is empty.

I glance at the clock. It's five minutes past seven. We have to hurry.

"Beatrice," I say, suddenly nervous, "I'd like to go for an evening stroll. Would you accompany me?"

"Sure," she says, pushing her chair back to get up. "I wouldn't mind getting some fresh air."

As we walk out the front door, she leans in and kisses me on the cheek. I remind myself that I am lucky that someone like her has taken an interest in me. Her left hand grabs my limp right hand. The first time she did that I felt so self-conscious that tears welled up in my eyes. I could feel her skin against mine, but I couldn't squeeze her hand to show her my pleasure. Now, after almost a year of her touching me in this way, I no longer flinch.

My neighbors wave at me as we walk by. I nod at them and smile. As we stroll down the cobblestone road, I long for the river quarter of my childhood. It used to be the most beautiful part of Cardiff before the big city dwellers came here and demolished it to build their luxury homes. Now, no one has a view of the Shenandoa, unless their house sits directly on the road running parallel to the riverbank. Almost all of the new houses share common walls with their neighbors, turning the quarter into one congested mass of bricks and concrete.

When I was a child, there were parks with small fields of grass for the children to play, and the houses stood apart and alone. Each one was built and rebuilt on top of foundations laid by our ancestors centuries ago. Each one was erected to be low and small so that every home had a view of the river and the mountains. Cardiff is one of the oldest Europan towns in Constantina, a fact that fills me with great pride. But the city-dwellers dug up those old foundations. When they threw away the old bricks, they tossed out our history along with them.

I avoid walking through the river quarter. Luckily there are other paths to the waters. On the northern outskirts of Cardiff, there is a small hill, Mending Spinney, where an ancient grove of trees still stands. My grandmother told me that the native people who helped my ancestors establish Cardiff showed them special powers possessed by the trees in the grove. I loved this one particular story Grandmother used to narrate often.

One day, Josiah, the only son of the founder of Cardiff, contracted the chills. That is what malaria was called when Constantina was first settled in the 1600s. Josiah was a sturdy young man of sixteen. In those days, healers from the native tribes used to come to Cardiff to treat the sick and dying. It so happened that, on that particular day, a young native woman named Soqi arrived in our small town. She was a healer's apprentice and took a liking to Josiah. She carried him to the grove of trees on the hill in the north. There she laid him on the grasses beneath an old maple tree and three times each day fed him the medicines she prepared from the barks and flowers of the plants in that grove. Within seven days, Josiah fully recovered, even though the chills rarely spared anyone's life in those early days. This is how the grove came to be known as Mending Spinney.

A few short weeks thereafter, Josiah asked Soqi to marry him in that grove just as the sun was about to set. She accepted his proposal, and they married in the way of her people and his, the Kunish. They lived happily together for many years and had two daughters and a son. One evening, when both of them were old, Josiah and Soqi sat in Mending Spinney, overlooking the Shenandoa below. The full moon was reflected in the waters when Soqi turned to Josiah and told him that it was time for her to join her ancestors. Not able to imagine greeting the next day without his beloved, Josiah asked her to take him with her. And so she held his hand in hers and placed his left palm on the bark of the old maple tree, putting her right palm next to his.

In the morning, when their children came to look for them, nothing remained except their palm prints in the bark of the old maple tree.

Every time I remember the story of Soqi and Josiah, I smile. Not many in Cardiff know of this story. In fact, Grandmother was one of the few in her generation who told it. And she passed the story down to Mother and to me. It is my secret knowledge, one that I carry in my heart. Whenever I have sought solace, I have sat in Mending Spinney and gazed upon the Shenandoa below. Never have I taken anyone there.

"Where are we going?" Beatrice asks me with uncharacteristic wonder as we approach the river.

"To a special place," I say with a smile.

We climb the little hill and enter the grove. The old maple tree still stands after almost four hundred years. And it doesn't take much imagination to see the palm prints of my ancestors. The sun is about to dip beneath the old mountains west of the Shenandoa. I lead Beatrice to a clearing from where we can enjoy the breathtaking view. For several moments we stand, looking down at the river, like Soqi and

Josiah must have done many centuries ago. Beatrice holds my right hand in both of hers and leans into me, her cheek touching mine.

"Bunim," Beatrice whispers, "I know I upset you often."

"Beatrice," I interject, not wanting to spoil the moment.

"No, please let me finish. I've never met anyone like you before. You're so patient and caring. I wish I could be like you. Honestly, I do. But the demons inside me. You don't understand. They kick and shout. And I just…"

I feel her tears on my cheek as her voice trails away. These moments of vulnerable honesty are when she is most beautiful to me.

"I wish I could help you, my love," I say, trying not to succumb to tears myself.

"You do," she whispers. "Every day that you are still with me, every day that you don't abandon me."

Gently I disentangle myself from her and inhale sharply. With the help of my walking stick, I kneel in front of this woman who has endured so much. Carefully I place the walking stick to my side and dip my left hand into my coat pocket.

"My lovely Beatrice," I say as I clear my throat and hold out the simple gold ring that belonged to my grandmother. "I don't know what I've done to deserve you. I never imagined that one day a woman as intelligent and caring as you…"

"Oh, Bunim!" Beatrice exclaims, her face lighting up with eagerness. "Are you about to do what I think you are? Then don't forget beautiful!"

"Yes," I confess, smiling, "I never imagined that one day a woman as beautiful and intelligent and caring as you would take an interest in someone as flawed as I am. You have become a part of me now and I love you deeply. I can no longer imagine my life without you in it. So I beg of you, would you be my wife?"

"As long as you promise to finally take me to bed today!" she shouts enthusiastically.

I'm flattered, but nonetheless stunned by her answer. My astonishment must be apparent on my face, since her expression softens, and she helps me to my feet.

"Put the ring on my finger," she orders me playfully, thrusting the fourth finger of her left hand into my chest.

## LONGING

*Once again, time, you have ejected me unceremoniously from the past into the present. My essence as Maya has been severed from that of Bunim. It takes a few moments to regain my bearings. As I look across the table at Bunim, his eyes lock onto mine. Guilt washes through me, and I shift my gaze to my hands. How can I look at a man whose most private memories I have just invaded? If only I could control these forays into others. How appalled they would be if they knew.*

*"You must control your emotions," the Most Knowledgeable One would advise me.*

*How I have exerted myself. For years I have tried. How I have labored to not feel as much as I do, as intensely as I do, all to no avail.*

*Bunim is listening to the others speak. But I know that his thoughts are elsewhere. Elsewhen, to be exact. Anguish surges within him. A very particular anguish that echoes stirrings buried deep within me. His past tugs at me with an insistence I cannot resist. I apologize, Bunim, for invading your mind and your body. I am unable to restrain myself. My essence transforms into Bunim's and time carries me back again. I cease being Maya.*

*I am Bunim of the past, an hour after sunset on that same day two and a half years ago.*

Here we are sitting on my bed, her thighs almost touching mine. I am bathed in clammy apprehension as I convulsively massage my right hand with my left.

"Don't you desire me?" Beatrice demands.

"Of course I do, dearest," I mumble, though I can't bear to look at her.

"Well, then, what's the problem?"

"You know that I haven't..."

"Of course I do," she snaps. "It was your ridiculously antiquated notion that we shouldn't be intimate unless we're committed to each other. So now that we finally are, let's get on with it."

"Why are you in such a hurry?" I manage to turn my face, only to see hers ablaze with annoyance. "We have our whole lives ahead of us. Can't I just hold you?"

"No!" Beatrice explodes and then calms herself with great difficulty. "I mean, you've made me wait this long, honey. I don't want to wait any longer."

Her tone has changed completely. Her mood undergoes this kind of drastic transformation multiple times during a conversation. It's dizzying, actually. In the beginning I used to become befuddled and anxious. Now I've gotten used to it and barely react. She places one hand on my knee and pulls my face toward hers with the other. Whenever she kisses me, I lose my ability to think. I only sense. The touch of her soft lips. The taste of her tongue. The smell of her floral perfume. My eyes close automatically when she is so close to me. But when her hand abruptly finds the core of my manhood, my eyelids flutter open.

Above her flushed cheeks, her green eyes shine vividly. I would almost call their glow defiant. I hear my own breathing accelerating, while she remains unaffected. What kind of sorcery is this?

"Well, all your parts are functioning properly," she observes matter-of-factly.

Instantly I feel that she is mocking me. Her tone floods me with shame for having become aroused. I don't have any reference point. Do all men feel this powerless and distressed when they are with a woman? I don't understand what is happening to me. I don't understand my feelings. Being near her makes me desire her, but her words cause me shame. I don't know whether I want to make love with her or not.

"Oh, come on," she snaps. "What's the matter now? Do you need more encouragement?"

Suddenly, she leans over and begins unbuckling my belt.

"What are you doing?" I cry out in shock.

"Stand up," she orders.

"Why?"

"I'm trying to help you."

"But Beatrice," I whisper, shame almost drowning my courage, "I don't feel comfortable."

Beatrice laughs out loud. Not a happy laugh, but one bursting with ridicule.

"You feel uncomfortable?" she sneers. "How absurd! I'm a gorgeous woman. And well, look at you. You should be grateful that I want you to have sex with me."

"Grateful?" My shame intensifies and begins to turn to anger. "Are you bestowing some gift on me that I need to be grateful?"

I turn away from her and buckle my belt.

"What the demon are you doing?" she demands.

"I don't want to, Beatrice," I say, quietly but firmly. "Not like this."

"Not like what?" she asks belligerently.

"Without love, without tenderness."

"Are you a man or a woman?" she hisses, mocking me again.

I lean on my walking stick and rise to my feet. "I think it best that you leave."

Her expression changes instantly, first to bewilderment, and then to contrition. "Oh, come on, darling. You know I was only playing. It's just that, well, you've made me wait for so long."

She rises to her feet, too, and puts her arms around my neck, pulling my face to hers. She gazes into my eyes, looking for forgiveness, and kisses me deeply, with love and tenderness. These are the moments I live for. These are the moments I wait for, the moments that dissolve the pain of her hurtful words, words I know are born from her own pain. I kiss her back with passion. I lean my walking stick against the dresser and wrap my right arm around her back. She must sense my uncertainty, because she guides my left hand down the side of her body. I've never done this before. As my hand acquaints itself with the contours of her curves, I marvel at how perfect she is. And in that moment, I desire nothing else but to be even closer to her.

"Buni," a familiar voice barges into my newly awakened sensations.

This is why I didn't want her to come to my home. My arousal disappears, almost instantaneously. I extricate myself from her as gently as I can.

"What the demon!" she exclaims, visibly angry. "Now?"

"I must, dearest," I say softly, kissing her on the tip of her nose. "She needs me."

"And what about me?" she demands.

"I'm all she has, Beatrice," I whisper tremulously. "I'll return as soon as I can."

I grab the walking stick leaning against the dresser and leave the room, hoping that she'll still be there when I come back. I dare not look back to see the anger seething from her. Once outside the room, I quietly close the door behind me and close my eyes. I breathe deeply for several moments, trying to calm myself. Not from my arousal, but from the panicked anticipation of the shouting that I will have to endure as soon as I return. If she is still here. After a few moments, the anxious palpitations of my heart abate, and I force my thoughts to turn to something else. Anything else.

Ours is the oldest house in Cardiff. The first one, actually. Built by my ancestor, Cardiff Cardozo, the Founder of this frontier settlement. He built only one flight of stairs on the side of the house to access the lone room on the flat roof. The room that became mine after Grandmother passed away. I hurry down the stairs in the chilly darkness of the evening and enter the main floor through the front door. I pass the kitchen and walk into the bathroom, the only one in the house.

I take off my shirt, pants, socks, and shoes and strip down to my underwear. I then lather my hands, forearms, and face with soap for many moments. I rub and rub and rub, willing away anything I might be carrying on myself. I open the faucet just enough to bring about a steady stream of warm water and begin washing away the soap. I dry myself with a towel from the upper shelf of a cabinet that I keep locked and retrieve a pair of pants and a shirt from the lower shelf. I put on these clean clothes and a sterile set of syntho mask and gloves before walking into the bedroom that is directly adjacent to the bathroom.

"Buni." She is crying again. "They came to take me away."

"Who came, Mother?" I ask gently through my mask, sitting down next to her on the bed and stroking her forehead.

"Those men from your father's shop." The fear in her quivering voice sinks my heart. "Tell your father to come and read to me," she implores. "Tell him that I won't go with them."

In such moments, it's best not to remind her that Father died four years ago. I let her tell me what ails her as I keep comforting her.

"Mother, would you like me to comb your hair?" I ask her, because that is one of the only activities that seems to give her any sort of relief.

"With the comb your father made for me when we became engaged?" Her face lights up through the tears wetting her cheeks.

"Of course," I say, then lean over and pick up the old wooden comb from her nightstand.

She likes the comb to always be in the same place, in front of the small ceramic framed picture of her and Father on their wedding day. I help her to sit up, and when she is comfortable, I begin gently combing her grey hair. Her blue eyes are opaquely greyish now from cataracts. She refuses to let them be operated away. What a beautiful strong woman my mother was just a few years ago. How cruel of this disease to take her away from me like this. She was full of vigor and courage. And the most astute person I knew. Everyone in Cardiff knows her as the school principal. They still call her the principal. She loves that.

"Mother, tell me about the time when that most mischievous boy in your school, Nathan, placed a bagful of toads in the teachers' room," I say.

I like to encourage her to exercise her memory as often as possible. Often it works, but today she doesn't respond, even though she looks directly into my eyes. I ask her patiently several more times. But she simply stares at me. At least her crying has subsided. Suddenly her glance moves to my walking stick that I've leaned against her nightstand.

"You still have that, Buni?" she inquires, forgetting that she asked me this just a few hours ago.

"Of course, Mother," I assure her with a smile, careful never to lose patience.

"Do you remember how you got it?"

"Tell me the story."

She stares at me again, lapsing into the silences that have become so strangely characteristic of her condition. I ask her three or four more times to tell me the story.

"Which story?" she asks.

"The story about my walking stick, Mother."

"Did it rain again today?"

"How did I get the walking stick?"

"When your father was a young man, he was so handsome. The handsomest young man in Cardiff."

"Mother," I say, continuing to comb her hair, "do you remember the story of my walking stick?"

"When you were seven years old."

"What happened when I was seven, Mother?"

"He always wanted to be a carpenter. But your grandfather needed help in the shop."

"You were telling me about the time when I was seven years old," I prompt her gently.

"It was the healer from the village across the Shenandoa, high in the mountains."

"What was the healer's name?"

"You were ill," she recalls. She is becoming agitated, but I don't want to inhibit her speech, even though she is not following one train of thought. "Your legs and hands had become paralyzed. You couldn't breathe properly. The doctor told us that you would die soon."

"I had polio, didn't I, Mother?"

"I remember the first day I entered this house. It was right after I married your father."

I try to bring her back to her previous string of thought. "Mother, what happened after the doctor told you I would die?"

"Your father prayed and so did your grandmother. Day and night they prayed. But I was tired of God not listening to us. So I went in search of the healer."

Inwardly I sigh in relief. She has regained her sense of self. These moments are rare, but when they do happen, I cling to her every word, her every expression. Because this is the mother I had. Because this is how I wish to remember her.

"I borrowed the boat of one of your father's friends and rowed down the Shenandoa," she continues enthusiastically. "I was determined to fetch Healer Soqi from her village."

"Healer Soqi?" In these moments of her lucidity, I encourage her to recall as many of her memories as possible so that her brain can reform the connections it has lost.

"Not the Healer Soqi your forefather Josiah married," she laughs. "No, this was a different Healer Soqi, who belonged to the same native tribe."

The sound of her laugh, her clear, joyous laugh, inundates me simultaneously with happiness and melancholy. I long for my mother. Even though she lies here in front of me, this is not her. This is merely a shell of a human being. How terribly I miss her. How peculiarly tormenting it is to be with someone who is there but not there.

"I traveled for several days on foot after reaching a particular bend in the river I remembered," Mother says, continuing to recollect that day from so long ago. "I climbed the mountain and slept under ancient pine trees. Just before sunset on the fourth day, I reached her village and asked her to come and save you from death. Even though she was over eighty years old, she was agile and alert. I followed her as she strode through the forest with the help of her walking stick. She gathered various types of bark and leaves and flowers and wrapped them carefully in cloth woven from tall grasses. Soon we returned to Cardiff. She tended to you continuously for seven days and six nights."

"I remember Healer Soqi, Mother," I say, tears beginning to well up in my eyes. "I remember waves of strength coming toward me as she sat next to me."

"She never left your side, my son," Mother says. "She told us that she had removed the virus. She had been able to heal the paralysis in most of your body but could not help your right hand and your left leg. You looked so forlorn that you would never be able to run again that she gave you her walking stick. Do you remember what she said, Buni?"

"Here, my child," I recall Healer Soqi's words to me from almost thirty-nine years ago, "I give you the walking stick my great-great-grandfather carved for my great-great-grandmother from the wise hickory tree that lives deep in the forest near our village. This walking stick has healing powers that shall strengthen your left leg as you grow. But you must focus your mind on your leg and endure the pain."

"Indeed, my son," Mother sighs. "Your father, may he rest in peace in heaven, thanked her profusely and offered to give her provisions in exchange for her kindness. She accepted nothing apart from a ride across the river."

"But Father didn't let her leave empty-handed, did he, Mother?" I have heard this story many times but feel genuinely excited each time she tells it.

"No," Mother says, smiling again. "Your father made her promise to stay for supper on her last day here, while he left for Mending Spinney. He told me later that he had noticed a large branch lying on the grasses of the grove. It had broken off of the ancient maple tree. When he returned to our house later that evening, he brought with him a part of that branch. He had carved the maple into a beautiful walking stick, to replace the hickory one Healer Soqi gave you. I remember how graciously she accepted his humble offering."

I look with great fondness at the hickory walking stick that has been my companion since childhood. How lucky I am to have such a strong mother. I continue combing her thinning hair as she lapses into silence once more.

"Mother?" I say, but she lays down on the bed and goes silent.

I place the comb on the nightstand, exactly how she likes it to be. She has already fallen asleep. Quietly I take my walking stick and leave her room to head into the bathroom. After I remove and fold my visiting clothes, I stack them again neatly in the cabinet, which I lock.

Then I discard the syntho mask and gloves and put on the clothes I was wearing before.

I leave the main floor through the front door. As I stand outside in front of the stairs leading up to Beatrice, I stare westward to the mountains. For several moments I breathe, locking in these new memories of Mother being lucid, of her smiling and laughing. Like Mother of before. I sigh and begin climbing the stairs.

*Time, I am grateful to you for giving me a brief respite from the past, allowing me to be in my own mind as Maya in the present once more. Out of the corner of my eye, I steal a glance at the Director of SAFE. What a noble man he is. What a soft, kind-hearted human being. How unselfishly caring he is. But how unfortunate also. For it is the goodness in others that tortured people like Beatrice seek out to exorcise their internal demons with and destroy. My heart weeps at the abuse he allowed himself to endure from her. I do not ask why, because I know why. When you are an empath and a broken person begs you for love, you move mountains to provide that love, no matter what the cost to you. When the one you love tells you over and over that you are flawed and weak and unworthy, you begin to believe it. Poor Bunim. He did not deserve to be treated that way. No one deserves to be treated with such disrespect and ridicule, no matter what.*

*I gaze at the faces of the men and women seated at this table in the Governor's Mansion. How little I know of most of them. In the wake of atrocious acts that harm life, it is truly difficult to still oneself long enough to consider the essence of the actor. To contemplate his childhood and experiences. To ask oneself what drives him to think and act in the way he does. When I remember to allay the ripples of my emotions long enough to truly consider others, I discern the motivations for their behaviors.*

*But I have always struggled with that. Even upon familiarizing myself with the tribulations and conflicts of another, I still find acts that harm others unforgivable. I cannot reconcile myself to the outcomes of such comportment. Bunim loses himself once more in his memories. I tremble at the anxious thoughts that drown him.*

*And me along with him. Time, you sweep me again into your arms and my essence merges into that of Bunim.*

*I am Bunim of the past, mere moments after he stood at the foot of the stairs gazing westward to the mountains.*

As soon as I close the door behind me, my clamminess returns. The peace I felt just moments before evades me. Beatrice is still here, but she is upset. Very upset.

"Where the demon have you been?" she demands loudly.

"Please, dearest," I whisper, not moving from the door. "Mother has just gone to sleep."

"Look, Bunim. I'm the most important woman in your life now. You've made it official. You can't just run off whenever she calls you."

"I am her son, Beatrice." My heart threatens to choke. "I am her only child. There is no one but me to take care of her."

"Nonsense! What are nursing facilities for? I'm sure I can pull some strings and get her into one in Robinson. We'll move into the place you already have there. Then you can go visit her once a month."

The only reason my knees don't buckle is that she has made this suggestion to me before. I inhale deeply and remind myself that she has never known a mother and so doesn't understand the love a child feels for the one who gave him life. Beatrice rises from the bed and walks toward me. Her mood has changed again. Now she is seductive. She kisses me deeply and leads me to the bed. As she undresses me, I let the tumult of emotions surge in alternating waves through me. Arousal. Love. Shame. Fear. Excitement. Frustration. Helplessness. Sadness.

It's strange. I've never had any such experience before with a woman. But how can it be that I am completely naked and she still has her dress on? It's not difficult for her to get my body to do what she wishes for it to do. Everything is too rushed for me to know what I desire in this moment. But I sense again that I am uncomfortable, that I do not want this. Not in this moment. I don't know how to voice these concerns. I already tried speaking out once. I don't know how to tell her that I don't want to face her anger again, especially not as she touches me intimately. I don't want to be ridiculed and shamed again. So I keep quiet and swallow my body's distress. I force myself to endure what she is doing to me as shame devours me for not feeling any pleasure.

She sits on top of me, astride my hips. I look at her face as she moves against me. But she stares out the window, her features expressionless. I want to say something to her. I want to call her to me. I feel so lonely in this moment. Lonelier than I have ever felt. As I climax within her without wishing to, the sadness that fills me is so immense that it spills out from my eyes onto my face.

When it's over, she sits still for several moments, her eyes closed. I can feel her contract around me. If I had any experience at all, perhaps I would understand what she is doing. But I don't. In one fluid motion she gets off of me. Wordlessly she puts on her panties and adjusts her dress and her hair.

"Beatrice," I say, my voice feeble, "you're not leaving, are you?"

"Of course, I am, Bunim." Her tone is brusque, her hand already on the doorknob, my grandmother's gold ring glistening on her finger. "See you later."

# CHAPTER FIVE

# EDGE OF LIFE

## EXPERIMENT

*Time, you catapult me back into the present. My body trembles. Even though my mind is no longer molded to Bunim's, I am certain that my heart palpitates as erratically as his. I feel exposed, as though he were the one who invaded me. Whom is it that I feel pity for? Him or me? Whose loneliness am I enduring in this moment? His or mine? I whisper to my body that nothing is the matter. I try to convince it that it is nestled in the cold safety of a plastic chair in a room full of people.*

*I cannot look at him. For I am filled with his shame, as well as mine. Even though I know that the shame should not be ours. If only you would let me forget, time. If only you would let me live in peace in this chain of Cause and Effect. I cannot calm the panic that has ensnared my body. How cruel of her. How unfeelingly cold. It must have been awful for him to endure such humiliation. No. I know that it was horrendous for him. How are people capable of such coldness? Do they not have hearts? Do they not feel? My breathing has become shallow. I must pull myself together. I cannot. I cannot. I feel like screaming. And so I open my mouth.*

*Suddenly, I feel Xetal's fingers around my wrist. Her calm flows into me. I close my mouth and eyes. Breathe in. Breathe out. Breathe in. Breathe out. Xetal continues to hold my wrist for many moments, until my breathing is no longer labored. Until I am stable enough to flow my gratitude into her. I open my eyes and look across the table.*

*Williams Fort.*

*Suddenly I hear someone at the table utter the name of this town. A heated discourse follows. But soon I do not hear their words. For my own memories of the first time I set foot in that historical border town block out all external sound. Time, I have anticipated what you are about to do. You are taking me back into my own self.*

*I am Maya of my past, half a month after the summer solstice of the year past.*

The sun has not yet risen. In the twilight I walk toward the abandoned structure of brick in yet another one of their frontier towns. They named this one Williams Fort. It is an old town in the northwestern part of Constantina, at the juncture of three different arms of the Potomac River. As I look upon the ruins of the fort, I wonder to myself why frontier towns can't be towns of peace. Obviously, the fort was erected for military purposes. Did they believe at the time that they could expand their borders from here?

Where is Xetal? She was supposed to meet me in the thicket on the southern side of the old fort. I survey the small patch of green, a rarity in Constantina. They seem to have an aversion to trees. They cut them down wherever they stand, no matter how ancient or powerful. I shake my head. In their ignorance, they don't even know that a tree contains power, let alone how magnificently far-reaching this power can be. A wide stump looks forlorn amongst the thin trees. I sit down on the edge of the stump and wonder what awaits us inside the fort.

"Arye," Xetal calls out to me, using an old word of our people meaning teacher, as she steps out from behind a tree.

"Xetal," I whisper, in case someone might hear us, "did Mother Nuna tell you anything more about the fort?"

"No," Xetal says, approaching me carefully. "She knows only that there is a great disturbance within."

I rise to my feet. "How does she know?"

"The healer from Keme's village shared this knowledge with Mother Nuna."

"Keme's village is nearby?"

"Yes, the village of his wife is within two days' walk."

"We must not be seen, Xetal."

"Fear not, Arye. I shall take you through an underground passageway of which the Constantinans do not know."

Less than thirty minutes later, we stand in a damp and dark brick-lined corridor below the earth.

"Just beyond that wall are the underground dungeons," Xetal whispers.

"Is there a door? Or do we have to…"

"There is a door," Xetal says as she wipes the wall in front of us with her hand. "It is merely hidden behind layers of dirt."

After several swipes of her hand, a door with a small indentation is revealed. Xetal inserts her fingers into the hole and tries to pull the door. It does not budge. She tries again, but with no luck. I gesture for her to step aside. I turn my right palm upward and focus my mind. Soon a small vortex of air appears above my hand. As it increases in size, I direct it to the door. Eddies surround the door and disappear into it. Within moments the door unlatches and swings very slightly toward us.

I direct the eddies back to my hand, where I focus them into a shimmering sphere. Soon the zephyrs expand and begin to engulf us.

"Stay close to me, Xetal," I whisper, ensuring that the sphere of concealment completely surrounds us. "We must not be seen."

I open the door wide so that there is enough space for both of us to pass through. The moment we step over the threshold into a large cavernous space carved out of the intestines of the earth, our senses become inundated. The stench of rotting human flesh and aging excrement slaps me in the face, nauseating me. I am utterly disoriented until my eyes adjust to the darkness and wish just as quickly that they hadn't. I see two rows of cells on both sides of a central earthen corridor. Solid iron bars, pockmarked and rusted, separate the cells from each other. And within the cells are hundreds of men and women and children moaning in pain, hanging on to life. Dying. Dead.

It takes a few moments for the ghastly sight to sink in for Xetal. She gasps and sinks to the floor, pale horror replacing the blood in her face. I kneel next to her on the damp earth.

"Xetal, rise to your feet."

"I cannot," she says, barely able to speak. "What abomination is this, Arye? Who has caged these human beings in this manner? How…"

Terror has rendered her speechless as she stares into the cells. Luckily for me, instead of dread, a deafening anger has been kindled within, rescuing me from yielding to despair.

"Xetal," I say, grabbing her by her upper arms and lifting her firmly to her feet, "we cannot help them if we do not know what happened to them."

Tears stream down her cheeks as she stares straight ahead, unable to hear me through her shock. I must reach her a different way.

"I need your help," I say, looking directly into her elongated brown eyes as I hold her face in both of my palms. "You are connected to water much more strongly than I am. I need you to taste the mist about them. I need you to discern what is ailing them."

"I cannot," she mumbles.

I, too, cannot help her in that moment, for the only thing that I could flow into her would be my outrage at what is around us. I breathe deeply. But the fetid smell makes me nauseous.

Trying to swallow my nausea, I plead again, "I need your help."

"I have never witnessed such horror, Arye," she whispers as she stares unseeingly into my face.

I inhale once more, this time focusing all of my energy on subduing my sense of smell. "Out of ignorance, humans can perform unspeakable atrocities. It is a sad reality."

"But our people never…" She cannot finish her thought.

"We aspire to fill our ignorance as much as possible with knowledge."

"And they do not?"

"No, Xetal. They do not."

Pity has replaced the anger within me. And pity is an emotion I can overcome easily. I close my eyes and empty my mind of pity, anger. Everything negative. I direct thoughts of hope and optimism through my palms to Xetal's face, into her being.

The dullness that had been dampening her luminous young heart begins to recede from her eyes, filling instead with resolve. "Then we must dissipate their ignorance, Arye. We must help them."

I sigh in relief and release her face. "I need you to taste the mist, Xetal. And tell me of the story it tells."

We walk closer to one of the cells. No one sees us as we continue to be camouflaged by vortices of air.

We notice a dark-skinned middle-aged woman lying on her back on the floor. "Brother," she whispers feebly, "look after my sons when I am gone."

A muscled man in tattered clothes, sitting against the iron rods, speaks between strained breaths. "I won't let you die, Ithbar," he says. "We are sons and daughters of Afrika. We will not be vanquished in this way."

The woman can barely keep her eyes open. "I cannot endure this pain much longer."

"You must, sister," the man replies in a deep voice.

"If it were merely pain of the body, perhaps I could withstand it," the woman moans, breathing heavily. "But this humiliation cleaves my heart."

"Let your thoughts dwell on the courage of the Revered Pool and you will be able to withstand even this humiliation that has been foisted upon us."

"Brother..."

"Yes, sister."

"Look after my sons when I am gone."

"Kasin," a man in the adjacent cell cries out, grabbing the bars against which the man with the deep voice leans, "why did you agree to let them do this to us?"

"What are you talking about, Mefu?"

"You let them do this to us."

"We all voted, Mefu," Kasin says, holding as still as possible to minimize the effort it takes to breathe. "You voted for this too."

"I was wrong!" the bare-chested man shouts. "It would have been better to have lost our homes than to endure this inhumanity."

"Don't be a fool!" Kasin bellows, coughing blood from agitation. "Would you have our people wander the streets like beggars and sleep defenseless on the streets? All while the pale men rest comfortably in the houses our forefathers built with their bare hands? Is that how the Revered Pool teaches us to conduct ourselves?"

Mefu stares defiantly at Kasin but remains quiet.

"Brother," Ithbar gasps in pain, "do not excite yourself."

"How can I not, sister? Is this a way to treat one's fellow man?"

"You must save your strength to fight what they have injected into us, brother."

Kasin looks down at the inside of his wrists. I follow his gaze and almost scream in horror. Just in time, I remind myself that no one must know of our presence. I look more closely at Kasin's arms. Scab upon scab has formed over wounds that have not had time to heal. Even now his blood trickles out from the long knife cut on his right wrist.

"Some of us are not that lucky, sister," Kasin sneers. "The injections are to test if their drugs work slowly."

"They injected me," Ithbar says quietly.

"Yes, I am relieved that they injected you," Kasin says, smiling weakly. "I am relieved that they did not take a knife to your body. For the slashes across our skin to pierce our blood directly are to test if their drugs work instantly."

"If only their drugs would kill me quickly," Mefu groans as pus leaks out from his wrist wounds, "instead of prolonging my suffering."

"We are strong, Mefu," Kasin declares with pride. "Like our fathers and their fathers before them. We must live according to the teachings of the Revered Pool."

"For in adversity is when your courage is tested," Mefu, Kasin, and Ithbar recite together.

I steady myself so that grief does not rob me of my ability to think. If they are not dying from what they have been injected and stabbed with, then they are dying from the infections their wounds and these horrid conditions in this dungeon are causing. They are sitting and lying in their own feces and urine. Only the strongest of men and women could endure such hardship and indignity. I fight tears of outrage from drowning my heart.

Xetal is unable to stem the tide of her sorrow. I must be strong for both of us. Once more I subdue my sense of smell and breathe deeply to kindle at least a memory of hope. I hold her hands in mine and close my eyes, pushing a surge of my optimism into her. When she opens her eyes, she appears calmer.

"Can you taste the mist, Xetal?" I ask her.

"The mist around them is heavy, Arye," Xetal says quietly.

"With the virus?"

"Yes, but not merely the virus."

"What, Xetal?"

"I cannot discern it."

"Focus your mind."

"It is of no use, Arye," Xetal sighs. "There is so much suffering here that I cannot distinguish the causes in the mist."

I stare into Xetal's face and wonder if the air is afflicted by the same strain of too many causes that I would be unable to distinguish one from the other.

"You fear that the air is similarly burdened?" she enquires.

"Yes."

I close my eyes for several moments and clear my mind. And so I stand until I smell nothing. Until I taste nothing. Until I see nothing. Until I touch nothing. Until I hear nothing. And in those moments free of sensory inputs, my thoughts become clear. Slowly I open my eyes.

I crouch down on the earthen floor and lay both my palms flat on the ground. As I close my eyes again, I let the earth connect me to everything that touches it. Feet, backs, hands, faces, heads, thighs, arms, wrists. I sense death and life and disease. I sense hope and despair and courage and fear. And I sense destruction that is caused by man.

"Who is responsible for this, Kasin?" Mefu demands.

"You know who, Mefu," the other man answers quietly. "So why do you waste your strength asking me."

"But which man is responsible?"

Kasin takes his time to respond. "I do not know."

"We must seek him," Mefu says, too weak to speak loudly.

"I will seek him," Kasin promises. "And when I know his name, I will make sure he experiences the consequences of the suffering he has caused."

I withdraw my hands from the earth and rise to my feet.

"Have you discerned the cause, Arye?" Xetal whispers.

"Yes, I have." A somber shadow casts itself on my being.

"Is there something we can do now to counteract it?"

"No, Xetal," I murmur, my voice breaking.

"But your powers are greater than mine, Arye," she pleads.

The sister of Kasin begins to cough uncontrollably. Kasin reaches out to comfort her. But between them lie the bodies of three dead men. And Kasin lacks the strength to move them aside to get to his sister. Ithbar finally stops coughing. For several moments she hyperventilates, but then resumes breathing with less difficulty.

"But why, brother," she gasps, "why are they doing this to us Afrikans?"

"Sadly, sister, we are not the only ones who are being made to suffer. When they were bringing us here, I saw Chin in the truck behind us."

Ithbar repeats her question. "Why are they doing this to us all?"

"So that they can find a way to treat their sick."

"But most of us never even caught the virus," Ithbar says, her pain audible.

"That is why they injected us with the virus first," Mefu says bitterly. "How else would they know if the drugs they pump into us bring death or life?"

"Death for most of us," Kasin says, closing his eyes. "Profit for a few."

Xetal turns to me and implores, "If we have the ability to relieve them of their suffering, we must do so."

I remain silent.

"They are innocent, Arye," Xetal pleads more ardently. "Do you not see? The Constantinans are conducting experiments on them to find a treatment for the pandemic."

"But Xetal," I ponder as I speak, "who shall weigh the long-term consequences if we intervene?"

## GRIEF

*On this occasion I thank you, time, for bringing me back into the present. What I witnessed that day inside the dungeons of Williams Fort was reprehensible beyond most of what I have experienced. In any chain of Cause and Effect. Even now I feel nausea rising into my mouth. The stench of that place lingers in my nostrils. A stench that was brought about by the expression of the darkest part of humans. I must not vomit.*

*I look into the faces of the people sitting across from me. I wonder how many of them actually saw and smelled what I did that day. If they had, would we all be sitting here today at this cold table, facing a potential course of action that might irreversibly alter the trajectory of all of humanity? Did those of them that ordered the Afrikans and the Chin to be transported like chattel to the death camps know to what they would be subjected? Did they care? They must have understood the depravity of their actions, for they did not subject any people of Europan descent to those horrors.*

*I lower my gaze, for I cannot bear to look at anyone in this moment. I fight to keep my bile down. I must focus elsewhen. I must distract myself with something here, now. But with what? Here we sit, at the precipice of potential disaster, and I am seeking distraction. I feel my sanity slipping away from me. Time, take me. I beg of you. Pull me to a different point in the matrix of Cause and Effect. No, I must muster strength and courage myself so that I can face adversity. I inhale deeply, trying not to remember the stench. I am not there, I mutter to myself in my mind. I am not there.*

*Suddenly I sense overwhelming misery from Bunim. When I open my eyes, I see that the blood has drained from his face. His grief is more acute than mine, sharper than that of any of the others in this room at this moment. He is recalling events of the same day half a month after the summer solstice of the year past. I know because my mind has latched on to his. Take pity on me, time, take me away. Any time is better than the present. Bunim, I apologize for invading your mind and your body once more. I am unable to control myself. My essence transforms into his.*

*I am Bunim of the past.*

Mother has been unable to breathe for several days. The doctor tells me that she will not survive the morning. I sit at the edge of her bed, stroking her back to ease the burden of her lungs as she lies on her right side, facing me. Her eyes are closed. It's better that way, because then she won't see the tears rolling down my cheeks. A sob escapes my lips. Too late, the sound follows.

"Buni?" Mother calls to me.

I wipe my face with my hands. There is no mask. There are no gloves. They can no longer protect her.

"Buni?" Mother opens her eyes and looks directly into my face. "Why are you crying, you silly boy?"

"Mother," I burst out, "I'm so sorry. I'm so sorry."

"About what, my dear son?"

What irony that she is lucid now, today of all days.

"I tried to protect you, Mother. It's my fault."

"Listen to me, Buni," Mother tells me sternly in between labored breaths. "This pandemic is not your doing. You would be prideful if you thought so. Remember that pride is a sin."

"But I failed you, Mother," I sob unabashedly.

"I lived the life I chose to live," she says, smiling. "With a man I loved more than I have ever loved God even."

My expression must have given me away, for Mother chuckles.

"I know that it's a sin to love anyone more than God. But your father was my life. The only reason I held on as long as I have is because of you, my son."

"Mother," I implore, trying to control my tears, "please don't leave me. You are the only person who knows me and loves me for who I am."

"Foolish boy, how can a mother be with her son his whole life? Did I not teach you to be self-reliant? Did I not teach you to love yourself without vanity?"

"Yes, Mother. You did."

"Then always remember, my Buni," she murmurs. Her eyelids close, but she summons the strength to open them again. "Remember that you must not give away your happiness to anyone. Always hold your happiness in your own chest. Protect your own happiness."

"What will I do without you?" I can barely form the words with my lips.

"You must live a life of honor, my son," Mother whispers. "For it is only honor that will save us now."

Her voice fades. Her eyes close. She drifts into sleep. I do not try to wake her, for I know that she is in pain when she is awake. As I gaze into her face, I can't help but rebuke myself. I know that this is my fault. I've played the past few days over and over in my thoughts. I am overcome with sadness as I remember for the hundredth time the events that transpired on the day of the summer solstice.

Beatrice stormed into my house unannounced that day, in a worse mood than usual. I was in the kitchen, preparing dinner for Mother.

"What is wrong with you?" she screamed at me.

"Beatrice, please don't shout," I pleaded.

"I'll shout if I want," she snapped. "What's your problem, Bunim? Aren't you even man enough to give me a baby?"

"What?" I was stunned by her question. "You told me that you were taking contraceptives."

"That's not the point! What kind of pathetic cripple are you?"

Beatrice had been cruel to me many times in the more than two years that we had been together. But she had never called me a cripple before that day. I found myself thinking that I could not forgive her for throwing that word at me.

"Beatrice," I said, my face drained of all color, "that is not the way to talk to me or any human being."

"I'll talk any way I like to whoever I like!" she yelled.

"Please lower your voice. Mother will become agitated."

"I don't give a damn if your mother becomes agitated. In fact, I'm going to tell her right now what a loser her son is."

She headed with determination to the bedroom. I followed her as quickly as I could with my walking stick.

"Beatrice, please, you mustn't go in there. You know that the virus is highly contagious. She can't be exposed to it."

"You go in there all the time," she shot back. "In fact, you've left me many times in the middle of a conversation, just because she calls you once."

Somehow I managed to reach the bedroom door before her and stand in front of it.

"I follow a very strict hygiene protocol every time I enter her bedroom and come in contact with her," I explained. "Please, Beatrice, you must not enter."

"Don't ever tell me what to do!" she shouted at me, knocking the walking stick out of my hand and shoving me aside.

I still remember my humiliation on that day as I fell to the floor and watched with dread as she opened the door to Mother's bedroom and entered. My mind returns abruptly to the present, for Mother is gasping for breath.

"Mother," I say, rubbing her back vigorously, "take long breaths."

Her breathing remains labored. So I lean over to the oxygen tank anchored to the wall between the nightstand and the bed. I dislodge the plastic mask and secure it over her nose and mouth before opening the valve on the tank. Gradually, her chest begins to heave less. I sigh in relief as I continue to rub her back with my right forearm.

Until recently, Mother would at least walk around the room for a few minutes as I held her hand. But she stopped leaving the bed several days ago, on the second of July, the last time I saw Beatrice. The last time we made love. She had been waiting for me on the top step of the stairs. She had made my favorite food, egg noodles with corn, which she fed me lovingly on my bed. Those moments are the ones I yearn for, wait for. When she is sweet, the whole world stops. I know only my love for her and forget all else.

Today is the ninth. I sit on the edge of Mother's bed. I don't remember sleeping much since Beatrice left that evening, a week ago. When I went downstairs to check on Mother that night, she had been gasping for air. I sent one of the neighborhood boys to fetch the doctor. He told me that the virus had invaded her lungs and that her chances of survival were almost non-existent.

I cannot fathom that, ultimately, I will be the cause of Mother's death and not this cruel neurodegenerative disease that has ailed her for so many grueling months. I should have never sought love and companionship with Beatrice. If I had not yielded to my loneliness, then Mother would still be well. I gaze mournfully at her face, the beauty contorted by age and disease. Suddenly she opens her eyes and looks directly into mine. I know that she wishes for me to remove the oxygen mask. So I do. Then she glances at the comb on her nightstand.

I pick up the comb and am about to touch it to her hair, when her eyes stop me.

"What should I do with the comb, Mother?" I ask gently.

Her gaze shifts to her left hand that is placed on the pillow close to her face. I understand. I open her fingers to place the comb between her palm and the pillow. She takes a deep breath and smiles at me, a smile that shines a bright light into the dark gloom of grief that smothers me. She then moves her gaze to the picture of her and Father. With the smile firmly on her face, she closes her eyes.

Father is no longer alone in heaven.

*Time, you cruelly transport me to the present long enough for me to see Bunim's eyes fill with tears. He wipes them away with the fingers of his left hand. I feel myself on the precipice of insanity, for I experience exactly what he does. Who am I in this moment? Am I Maya? Or am I Bunim, who just lost the woman who loved him most dearly because of the egotism of the woman he dared to love? I cannot extricate myself from him. As his memories awaken again, I drown once more within Bunim on that same day, merely a few hours later.*

*I am Bunim of the past.*

It is the evening of the ninth. It seems that the whole quarter has congregated in my house to pay respects to Mother. I am unable to mumble even a polite word of gratitude as I am showered with condolences. Despite the aid of my walking stick, I am unable to stand. So I sit on a chair near Mother's dead body, which has been placed in a clear plastic box to help stem the spread of the virus from her to others. I can barely look up.

It is several hours past twilight. The last visitor must have left the house, for I hear nothing except my own sorrow. I don't know how much time has passed, when I sense familiar vibrations on the floor. The vibrations stop. A floral perfume fills my nostrils instead.

"Mother is no more," I whisper. They are the first words I have spoken since I placed the comb in her hand this morning.

"I'm pregnant," Beatrice announces, her voice holding neither joy nor compassion.

I look up at her, glimmers of excitement knocking on the door of my grieving heart, asking for permission to enter. "We should get married as soon as the mourning period is over," I offer tremulously, tentatively imagining a possibility of happiness.

"I'm not going to marry you, old man," she declares. "But you will pay for maintaining me and this child. I'll have my lawyer send you the paperwork."

Her cold malice freezes my heartbeat. Before my lungs can begin functioning again, Beatrice walks toward the front door.

"Oh," she adds, throwing my grandmother's most prized possession, the only piece of jewelry she ever owned, at my feet. "Keep your cheap ring. I've never cared for it."

She slams the front door behind her on her way out. I look at Mother's face, still lit up in that smile from the morning. Her dead fingers clutch the comb Father carved for her from a fallen branch of the old maple tree when they first became engaged.

"I have loved only three women since I was a child," I say numbly to the corpse of my mother. "Grandmother, you, and Beatrice. I lost two of you on the same day. I have no more love to give, Mother. And so I vow never to love another woman again."

# GLIMPSES OF THE END

*Time, you have dissolved the past once more into the present. But in my shock at the cruelty with which Bunim was treated, I am oblivious to you now, time. My surroundings barely register. I am in a plastic chair, at a plastic table, in a room full of people sometimes shouting and sometimes speaking quietly. My essence has not extricated itself from his, for his unimaginable grief of that day, his screaming loneliness ruptures my insides.*

*I am Bunim of the present, stuck at this plastic table in this darkened office in the capital.*

Of all my memories of this building, one pricks me like a thorn. It was the day before the autumnal equinox of last year when I was sitting in the cafeteria of the Governor's Mansion, eating my midday meal. Shortly after Mother's death I had moved to Robinson, for I could not bear to be in our house without her. Two young women sat at the table in front of me. They were speaking loudly enough for me to hear.

"Did you hear about Beatrice Holden, the President's aide?" one of the women giggled.

"Oh, she's scandalous!" the other one exclaimed, relishing the gossip.

Both of them stole not-so-furtive glances at me before continuing with their conversation.

"She thinks she's God's gift to man."

"She's not that pretty."

"Maybe. But she does have a way with men, doesn't she? She knows how to wrap them tightly around her little finger."

"What did you hear?"

"Well, apparently she ensnared some old man and convinced him that she was pregnant with his child."

"She wasn't?"

"No, she faked it so that she could extort money from him."

"What a horrible woman!"

"But so clever."

*My essence separates itself from that of Bunim, who suppresses his remembered anguish. I am Maya once more. I look around me, into the faces of the twelve men and women still seated at this long, sterile table. We are all of us on the precipice of a course of action that shall have grave consequence for all of humanity. As the end of this Meeting of Conclusions nears, what shall be their choice?*

www.ingramcontent.com/pod-product-compliance
Lightning Source LLC
Chambersburg PA
CBHW030238180626
46810CB00008B/3189